Welcome to
February
9
1964

Beatles in America

February 9, 1964

Time Travel Simplified

A Curated Multimedia

Time Travel Experience

Mark Hatala, Ph.D.

Time Travel Press

All rights reserved under
International and Pan-American copyright conventions
Published in the United States of America
by the Time Travel Press
09 08 07 06 05 1 2 3 4 5

Beatles in America - February 9, 1964
Time Travel Simplified: A Curated Multimedia Time Travel Experience
by Mark Hatala, Ph.D.

ISBN-13: 978-1-933167-64-0
ISBN-10: 1-933167-64-5

Book Design: Charles Dunbar

The font used in this book is Times New Roman, with headings in Courier

To incorporate this book into your life experience, visit our website at
timetravelsimplified.com

Table of Contents

"The past is a foreign country; they do things differently there."
                                        - L. P. Hartley, *The Go-Between*

Days fly by in a blur, with one day seemingly like the next. But what if you could stop time, and examine one day in depth? Read the news from that day. Enjoy the print media. Watch television. See the commercials.

And what if you revisited that day over and over again - what insights would you take away about that day, and about yourself? That's the purpose of this book, and the promise of time travel. Quite simply, time travel is a "magic well" - the more you draw out of it, the more there is to take.

We often think of time travel as we see it portrayed in science fiction or popular movies like the *Back to the Future* series. In these scenarios, a person steps into a "time machine" (which may or may not be a DeLorean automobile) and vanishes into another time. Once there, the person has to deal with the known "paradoxes" of time travel, such as avoiding altering the past in such a way that it negatively impacts the present (or future). They also have stereotypical views of the time they are travelling to.

That is NOT what this project is about. I have no physical "time machine" for you to step into to visit the past. That's not a problem though. Ironically, you have the time machine with you at all times, and the real paradox of time travel is not that time travel changes the past - it's that it changes you. Who you are. How you see the world. How you see the past and the present, and how you see yourself fitting into the greater human experience.

The ability to use your own critical analysis of what you've experienced in the past and apply it to your own time is the gift of time travel. Not only will you understand the past, you'll understand how we got to this particular present, and most importantly, you'll understand yourself - your hopes, fears, biases, influences, and ways of seeing the world - in an entirely new way. Time travel, at its core, is about human potential and personal growth.

This book examines February 9th 1964, the day that the Beatles made their American debut on *The Ed Sullivan Show*. While I didn't physically experience that day (I wouldn't be born for another two years), I have certainly been impacted by it, and have a lifelong love of the Beatles and each of the individual members - John, Paul, George, and Ringo.

My point is that it doesn't matter whether you've experienced a day in "reality" in order to understand it. Even historic events that I was an adult for, such as the attacks of September 11th, I'm sure I would interpret differently now.

My point is that it doesn't matter whether you've experienced a day in "reality" in order to understand it. Even historic events that I was an adult for, such as the attacks of September 11th, I'm sure I would interpret differently now.

Historians often say that when examining a particular historical event, we should forget what we know about it because people at the time didn't have any idea how things were going to turn out. This is an obvious fallacy, because in general, we DO know how things turned out. And what we don't know, we can research or look up online. This is our enormous advantage over people in the past. Call it the "time traveler's edge."

One of the goals of this time travel experience is to make you "fluent" in the American culture of February 1964, the world that the Beatles entered on that Sunday night. You will understand the major historical issues of the time through the eyes of the people living, writing, and acting in that time. You'll understand the inside jokes and the social trends. What is going to happen in the investigation of the assassination of JFK? The Civil Rights movement? The war in Vietnam? The Space Program? The Women's Liberation Movement? Youth culture? The "British Invasion" of popular music? These are the issues which dominated the media conversation of February 1964. Soon you'll see why.

This isn't a history of February 1964. Histories are written by people from a later era to explain an earlier era to people of their own time. Using the methodology developed for time travel simplified, you will see that the person from a later era explaining another era to you is you. You're not a historian. Or even a "time tourist" who visits and leaves.

You're a time traveler. Someone who understands the past because they've lived there.

This book is divided into four sections with research and learning modules throughout.

Setting the Stage is the first section, and the goal is to familiarize you with the zeitgeist ("spirit of the times") of February 1964. Most of the media is in print, and so this section has a large reading component. However, the visual media is also significant, and includes the pandemonium of the Beatles arrival in New York City on February 7th, their press conferences, and the "behind the scenes" footage of their first visit to America. Each source has several modules, and so there are 50+ modules for this section.

The Day is the second section, and it is all about the media from February 9th 1964. Since it was a Sunday, it begins with the morning newspapers, (the *New York Times* as well as the *New York Times Magazine*) and ends at 1030PM with the broadcast of *What's My Line* (I like to be in bed by 11!). In between is an entire day's worth of programming - movies, game shows, children's programming, reruns, and the complete primetime show schedule (shows like *Ozzie & Harriet*, *My Favorite Martian*, *The Wonderful World of Disney*, *Bonanza*, and the *Judy Garland Show*, in addition to the complete *Ed Sullivan Show*). The entire day of television and print media as people on that day experienced it. While you should take longer than a day to complete the 30+ modules dedicated to February 9th, you will understand that single day better than you do any other. That's time travel - simplified.

Debriefing is the third section, and it is significant in a few important ways. First, it includes the print media which came out right after February 9th, such as *Time*, *Newsweek*, and *Life* magazine. These are invaluable because they teach what the "gatekeepers" of the news media considered to be the important news from that week (HINT: The arrival of the Beatles was important!). Second, it includes retrospectives on the Beatles Ed Sullivan appearance. For example, performer Mitzi Gaynor discusses what it was like to have top billing over the Beatles! In other words, the Debriefing covers what the people who lived through the experience considered significant and important from the day after the event to four decades later.

I've also included a section in the Debriefing on What the Beatles Read (and Wrote), which provides examples of what we know (through photographs) the individual members were reading and writing about in 1964. For example, Paul reading a March 1964 comic book, Ringo reading a June 1964 copy of *Modern Screen*, and John's 1964 book *In His Own Write*.

The Background Research is the final section, and covers the cognitive science and memory research which explains why you'll remember February 9th 1964 as if you lived through it. Spoiler alert: it's because you did! That's the guarantee of the Time Travel Simplified methodology - it's time travel or it's free! It's not necessary to read this section in order to understand time travel, but it's there (with citations and references) if you're interested.

I want to close this introduction by welcoming you into our Society of Time Travelers. We've all shared a unique experience that we can talk about on the discussion forums at timetravelsimplified.com. Each of us brings a unique perspective to the past, and sharing it with others, especially fellow time travelers, is part of the reward. Thank you for joining me on this journey. Let's get started!

A note on accessing materials online

All of the print and visual media mentioned in this book are available online at timetravelsimplified.com - it's easy to access - just look for "February 9 1964" at the top of the page or click on the picture of the book. That will take you directly to the page with all of the modules.

I think that the material is most conveniently accessed via a tablet, laptop, or desktop computer. An advantage of a tablet is that many people are familiar with reading media or watching video on a tablet. Laptop and desktop computers are also good because the media is scaled to be easily read.

While I realize that many people (especially young people) read everything on their phones, I believe that the amount of material accessible on a phone doesn't lead to the best reading experience. However, that might be my own opinion! The modules are often presented out of order on the "February 9 1964" page when you use a phone to access the material. All the modules are still there, but you might have to hunt around to find the one you want.

Again, no matter how you're accessing the online materials, all of the modules, by number, can be accessed via the "February 9 1964" page.

A note about modules

There are blank spaces (and entire pages) throughout this book for you to write down your thoughts and reactions to the modules. While I go into more detail about this in the *Background Research* section, suffice it to say that recording your notes in your own handwriting within this book will enhance your time travel experience.

This isn't a "textbook" - it's a workbook!

14

Setting the Stage

This first section is dedicated to providing context for February 9th 1964, and so it begins with brief coverage of a major event immediately preceeding our date - the assassination of John F. Kennedy. Is it a coincidence that I'm also writing a Time Travel Simplified book about this particular date (November 22, 1963) and am trying to garner interest in the book? Perhaps.

We then move directly into February 1964, with a juxtaposition "women's magazines" and "men's magazines." So, *McCall's*, *Cosmopolitan*, *Screen Stories*, and *Good Housekeeping* for an idea of magazines aimed at women, and *Esquire*, *Playboy* (since none of the centerfold pictures are included, you can truly say that you are reading *Playboy* for the articles), and *Police Gazette* for men.

What was youth culture like in early 1964? For young women there's *Co-ed*, or as the tag line on the magazine says, "the high school magazine for homemakers and career girls." The next two magazines, *True Men* and *Guy*, provide a glimpse into the interests of young men of the time. The adolescent comedy of the time comes next, featuring selections from *Mad* magazine.

Cultural magazines are next, featuring *Ebony* and *Jet* (which were published primarily for an African-American audience) and *USSR: Soviet Life*, for a view of life under communism as the communists saw it in 1964.

Next come the news, business, and mainstream culture magazines - *Fortune* and *The Atlantic* - in order to understand the political, financial, and cultural spirit of the time.

The print media concludes with *Science Digest* to understand what the scientific interests of 1964 were like.

The visual media for this section include a Universal News newsreel from February 3rd and a video about "Two-Gun Pete," a police officer discussed in *Jet*.

While I have grouped the print and visual media in this way, you certainly don't have to, and can feel free to skip between the items you want to read or see first. In keeping with the methodology of Time Travel Simplified, you should complete the modules for this section (by writing them out in this book or just thinking about them) before moving onto the next section, which specifically examines the day the Beatles landed in New York - February 7th 1964. That includes footage of the Beatles arriving at their hotel and the issues of *Time* and *Life* that came out that day.

Enjoy!

JFK in Dallas - November 22, 1963

Module 1 - Kennedy's morning in Dallas - November 22, 1963
What are your thoughts as you watch this footage from the morning of November 22nd? What do you know already about the assassination of President Kennedy? Does this video change or enhance your knowledge of the event?

Time - November 22, 1963

Module 2 - The Presidency
President Kennedy "aged his Secret Service detail ten years" in the week prior to his assassination. What exactly did he do to accomplish that? And what was President Kennedy's primary political agenda in the week before his death?

Note: This particular *Time* magazine was delivered to Dr. Robert Guenther in Dallas, Texas on November 22, 1963! Dr. Guenther served as a Captain in the Army during World War II, and was awarded a Silver Star for his bravery at the Battle of the Bulge. After the war he practiced dentistry for 43 years, and passed away in 2004.

First Magazine for Women

February 196?
50 cents

McCall's

THE STEPMOTHER
& STEPFATHER
& STEPCHILD
A Revealing Study
of Their Very
Special Problems

ALL THE WORLD
LOVES PARIS!
12 Pages of
Spectacular
Photographs by
David Duncan

THE DIONNES
WRITE TO THE
FISCHER QUINTS

JUDY GARLAND'S
OWN STORY
The Last Heartbreak
Woke Her Up

MISS AMERICA'S
PATTERN
WARDROBE

BOYS & OTHER
BEASTS:
The Smart
New Guide to
Teen Dating

McCall's - February 1964

Although it began as a magazine called *The Queen* in 1873, McCall's grew to be one of the most popular magazines in America, billing itself as the "First Magazine for Women." Under the editorship of John Mack Carter, McCall's circulation in the early 1960s was 8.4 million a month - only *Reader's Digest* and *TV Guide* sold more copies.

So what happened? Cultural changes and a rapid turnover of editors. For example, journalist Shana Alexander (who would go on to become famous for her "Point/Counterpoint" segments on CBS's *60 Minutes*) was made editor in 1969. She had no experience as an editor, and said "I have to educate myself about women's magazines, but I think I know something about women." She was gone by 1971. By the 1980s *McCall's* began billing itself as "The Magazine for Suburban Women," but suburban women did not agree.

McCall's hit bottom in 2000 when Rosie O'Donnell was made the editor. She said "I want a magazine that celebrates real women, that understands that they care about more than waistlines or the latest makeup styles or fashions, that they want to be relevant and help each other and care about the world." In 2001 the name of the magazine was changed from *McCall's* to *Rosie*. It ceased publication in 2002.

Regardless, our February 1964 edition of *McCall's* is a great one, with the cover featuring a time-traveling January Jones from *Mad Men*. Just kidding! That's model Deborah Dixon! Born in Texas, she became an international model and was popular throughout the 1960s, even inspiring the song "Snow Queen of Texas."

There are five modules associated with this edition of McCall's. Complete any or all of them.

Module 3: Kubrick, Beatniks, and Beatles

The "Sight & Sound" section is pretty prescient in predicting the rise of filmmaker Stanley Kubrick, as well as the coming popularity of the Beatles. What qualities do you think stood out for either Kubrick or the Beatles which made their success seem preordained?

Module 4: Claire Boothe Luce

Claire Boothe Luce's column "Without Portfolio" is mostly just an opportunity for her to give her opinion on reader questions. If she is unfamiliar, suffice it to say that she was a writer, socialite, ambassador, and conservative anti-communist. For this module, what do you think about the idea of America's "prestige" in the world? Is it higher or lower than it was in 1964? Or is it just different? Why?

Module 5: Q & Advertising

This is an utterly unique monthly column where readers' questions about advertising are addressed. Which question and answer do you believe are the most relevant to our time? Why? And do you believe that advertising has changed, or is it still basically the same as it was in 1964?

Module 6: Frankly Speaking

Asking celebrities about their marriage proposals is a unique idea and reinforces the ethos of the time that adults should be married. Whose story do you find most interesting? Research whether the marriage they describe lasted.

Module 7: Judy Garland

This is a very personal account of where Judy Garland was in 1964, and is best read after watching the February 9th episode of her show. What do you feel is the most significant revelation in this piece? Why?

Module 8: Art Linkletter

Dedicated to the proposition that "Kids Say the Darndest Things," Art Linkletter's column is likely to bring a smile to anyone. Which is your favorite expression or illustration? Why? And do you think a column like this could be written today? Why or why not?

February 1964 · 35¢

COSMOPOLITAN

THEME OF THIS ISSUE: *THE MARRIED AND THE UNMARRIED*

THE ANATOMY

THE PLIGHT OF PRETTY GIRLS IN ENGLAND

Begum Aga Khan Tells Her Love Story

LILLIAN WHITE DEER
A CONDENSED NOVEL

Lolita meets up with
Mark Antony
in Mexico

SPECIAL
REPORT **PROFILE OF OUR FIRST LADY**

Cosmopolitan - February 1964

The *Cosmopolitan* magazine of 1964 is not much like the version we have today, with its usual monthly litany of sexual tricks to make your partner scream in ecstasy, celebrity interviews, weight loss advice, relationship quizzes, and astrology. The difference? Helen Gurley Brown, who edited *Cosmopolitan* for thirty-two years starting in 1965. She wrote the bestseller *Sex and the Single Girl* in 1962, and managed to turn *Cosmopolitan* into THE magazine for successful single women. As a firm believer in sexual liberation, she promoted the idea that single women should enjoy sex without any feelings of shame or guilt.

As a force to be reckoned with, Helen Gurley Brown still manages to make it into our February 1964 issue of *Cosmopolitan* in the article "Billion-Dollar War Between the Sexes," specifically for her *Lessons in Love* book, which "discourses about such matters as how to have an affair, how to talk to a man in bed, how to get a girl to the brink [!], and how to keep her this way if you're not going to marry her."

To provide a little history, *Cosmopolitan* started as a "family" magazine in 1886, but struggled until William Randolph Hearst bought it in 1905. Hearst brought in a host of famous writers including O. Henry, Sinclair Lewis, and Jack London, and by the 1930s *Cosmopolitan* became something of a literary magazine, with serials, novelettes, and short stories. However, by the early 1960s it was considered just another bland, boring, general interest magazine, albeit one that still published a lot of fiction. For example, our February 1964 issue contains three short stories and a condensed novel. But those aren't very interesting, and so aren't included in the three modules associated with this edition of *Cosmopolitan*.

Complete any or all of the modules.

Module 9: Three women in one

When LBJ unexpectedly came to the presidency in November 1963, he wasn't very well known at a national level, and even less was known about his family. While this is something of a "puff piece" about Lady Bird Johnson, it provides a glimpse into the expectations for women in 1964 - devoted wife, partner in politics, businesswoman. And that's not even including the fact that she's a mother! What aspects of her life do you find to be the most interesting?

Module 10: Anatomy of a family

When you consider that Family Services is called to intervene in a situation where a high school son is smoking, playing hooky, and occasionally stealing a bike or two, the early 1960s were clearly a different time in America. While this is an incredibly intimate story about family life and friction, how different do you feel it is from the issues of our own time? Would finding "an obscene, trashy book with a half-dressed woman on the cover" under a teenage son's pillow elicit the same reaction today? Finally, do you feel that a parent reading this article in 1964 would find their own family reflected in the Bennett's? Why or why not?

Module 11 - Marriage and sex in America

Marriage has never been easy, and this article covers the emerging field of marital counseling and sex education. The divorce rate in 1960 was 2.2 annual divorces for every 1,000 couples, and rose to 2.5 by 1965, and to 3.2 by 1969 (the divorce rate peaked in 1981 at 5.3), so marriages (or the idea of what marriage should look like) were becoming more fragile. How do you think relationship issues have changed from 1964 to our time? What are your thoughts about how "relationship" information should be presented to children and teens? Through their parents? Through the schools? Over the internet? And how do you believe this information has changed from the culture of 1964 to our time?

DELL
20 740 102

screen
stories

FEB. 35c

**Fabulous
New Star**

ELKE
SOMMER

*"—so Hot
She Sizzles!"*

NATALIE WOOD and
STEVE McQUEEN
in
**"Love with
the Proper Stranger"**

SOPHIA LOREN and MARCELLO MASTROIANNI
in "Yesterday, Today and Tomorrow"

Screen Stories - February 1964

Screen Stories was a Hollywood fan magazine published from 1948 to 1979. Our February 1964 edition features actress Elke Sommer on the cover. Originally from Germany, she became one of the most popular actresses of the 1960s. She was also a popular "pin-up girl" and had a pictorial in *Playboy* in September 1964!

I've included this edition of *Screen Stories* because it captures what was happening in the world of film in February 1964. There are five modules associated with this issue. Complete any or all of them.

Module 12: Mike Connolly's Exclusive Report from Hollywood
Mike Connolly wrote a gossip column for The Hollywood Reporter from 1951 until his death in 1966, and the most famous incident of his career occurred in June 1963, when actress Shirley MacLaine walked into his office and punched him in the face. She didn't like what he wrote about her career and favored direct action! What do you think is the most interesting Hollywood gossip in this column? For me, it's the Elvis date with Ann Margaret - how many bodyguards does Elvis need?!

Module 13: Yesterday, Today, and Tomorrow
This article is mostly a pictorial account of one of the three stories in the Best Foreign Language Academy Award-winning film Yesterday, Today, and Tomorrow, starring Sophia Loren and Marcello Mastroianni. However, it is mostly an opportunity to present photos of Sophia Loren! How are foreign-language films marketed in our time? Do you feel that they are more or less accessible to the public now than in 1964? Why or why not?

Module 14: Screen Picture Quiz
They're all locked up! Personally, I got none of these answers correct - maybe you can do better!

Module 15: What's Playing
I've included this in order to present the movies that were playing in theaters in February 1964. Many of them (if not all) have subsequently shown up on television and streaming services. How many have you seen? Which was your favorite? What would you say was the quality of film entertainment available to the public in February 1964?

Module 16: Advertising
The advertising in Screen Stories is very interesting! From the ads, who do you think was the target demographic of this magazine? And which advertisement is your favorite? Do you feel that any of the ads could be run during our time? Why or why not?

FEBRUARY 1964 • 50¢

Good Housekeeping

"THE AMERICAN WAY OF DEATH"

BY JESSICA MITFORD

Special condensation of the
hotly argued best-seller
that attacks showy,
extravagant funeral
practices

DR. JOYCE BROTHERS
BEGINS A SEARCHING
PERSONAL COLUMN

KNOW THE SYMPTOMS
THAT CAUSE FALSE
CANCER FEARS

"LIFE OF THE PARTY"
COOKBOOK—16 PAGES

Good Housekeeping - February 1964

Along with *McCall's*, *Good Housekeeping* was known as one of the "Seven Sisters" - a group of magazines targeted for married women whose primary occupation was homemaker. It is one of the three (along with *Better Homes and Gardens* and *Woman's Day*) that is still being published in our time. For better or worse, each of the others has ceased publishing, including *McCall's* (2002), *Ladies' Home Journal* (2016), *Redbook* (2019), and *Family Circle* (2019).

Good Housekeeping was a powerhouse in the early 1960s, with a circulation of 5 million copies per month. At least part of the success of the magazine can be attributed to the "Good Housekeeping Seal of Approval" which was initiated in 1909. As an early version of *Consumer Reports*, the Good Housekeeping Research Institute (GHRI) was created in 1902 as a way to test the products advertised in the magazine. To increase the credibility of the "Seal" granted by the GHRI, it was originally run by Harvey W. Wiley, the first appointed commissioner of the U.S. Food and Drug Administration (FDA). Products which were granted the Seal were backed by a two-year limited warranty for refund or replacement! However, after an investigation by the Federal Trade Commission (FTC), in 1962 Good Housekeeping changed the wording of the "Seal of Approval" to a guarantee of "Product or Performance," without validating the advertisers' claims about the product.

The February 1964 issue is an interesting one, with a lengthy condensation of Jessica Mitford's book *The American Way of Death*, which was an expose on the extravagant overcharging endemic in the funeral industry. While I don't have a module based on her book (the condensation is still too long and is now 50 years out-of-date), there are three modules associated with this issue of *Good Housekeeping*. Answer any or all of them.

Module 17: I thought I'd married a Momma's boy!

This is an interesting article on the relationship of a young married couple trying to cope with family issues, particularly with the author's mother-in-law. The couple married at 19 (for him) and a week over 18 (for her), with both of them having high school diplomas and jobs. How common of an arrangement would this be in our time? And do you believe that this is more of an issue from 1964, or do the issues with in-laws persist into our time? How are the issues the same or different? Why?

Module 18: Dr. Joyce Brothers

This is the very first monthly column by Dr. Joyce Brothers for *Good Housekeeping* - a column she would continue to write for the next 40(!) years. As a pioneer in the field of "popular" psychology, her writing was meant to be accessible to the general public. Her initial column is fascinating because it discusses what it means to be a "real womanly woman." How do you feel these expectations have changed since 1964? Or have they changed at all? Take the quiz she provides and score your answers! In what ways would this quiz remain valid in our time?

Module 19: When the Queen has a baby

In February 1964, Queen Elizabeth was pregnant with her fourth child, Prince Edward, who would be born on March 10th. What revelation did you find most interesting? For me it was that the Home Secretary had to be present at the birth of a royal child, either "behind a curtain or a half open door." And how do you think an article like this would be presented today?

FEBRUARY, 1964
PRICE 60c

Esquire
THE MAGAZINE FOR MEN

Fly to Europe with the stewardess of your choice (below). On the way, read p. 49

1 Effie Housman, El Al
2 Eliane Gottlieb, Air France
3 Nicole Savoye, Air France
4 Zarine Vakil, Air India
5 Pushpa Nangolwala, Air India
6 Krishna Mahtani, Air India
7 Nily Eisner, El Al
8 Runa Brynjolfsdottir, Icelandic
9 Hildur Hauksdottir, Icelandic
10 Stefanis Gudmundsdottir, Icelandic
11 Jill Wolff, BOAC
12 Helen D'Aquino, BOAC
13 Sherry Wing, BOAC
14 Albertina Castellani, Alitalia
15 Maria Monteforte, Alitalia
16 Maria Aspland, TWA
17 Joan Honold, TWA
18 Karin Krahmer, Lufthansa
19 Lillian Frizzoie, Pan American
20 May Yasuda, Pan American
21 Jill Edwards, SAS
22 Carlotta Gunther, Alitalia
23 Rose Marie Maisonet, Iberia
24 Mary Lynn McCutcheon, TWA
25 Patricia Price, TWA
26 Bonnie Friesth, TWA
27 Helga Schenk, Lufthansa
28 Barbara Brennan, Pan American
29 Karin Weber, Pan American
30 Anita Appelgren, SAS
31 Irene Hval, SAS
32 Sheila Hanlen, Irish Intl. Airlines
33 Una Madden, Irish Intl. Airlines
34 Thérèse Mutsh, Sabena
35 Danièle Vuylsteke, Sabena
36 Karin Sleidle, Lufthansa
37 Barbara Keller, Qantas
38 Annette Carswell, Pan American
39 Doris Hagmauer, Swissair
40 Marlen Menzi, Swissair

Esquire - February 1964

Started in October 1933 as an offshoot of the magazine *Apparel Arts* (which would become *Gentlemen's Quarterly* or *GQ*), *Esquire* was designed to be a sophisticated men's magazine which covered politics (the founders, Henry Jackson and David Smart, had very different political ideas), literature (they published works by Ernest Hemingway and F. Scott Fitzgerald), and men's fashion. Although it was initially intended to be published as a quarterly magazine and cost 50 cents an issue during the Depression (an inflation adjusted $10.15), *Esquire* proved to be so popular that it became a monthly.

Beginning with the second issue, a cartoon character named "Esky" graced the front cover in some form until he was retired in 1978. He remains present in our February 1964 edition as the dot in the "i" of "Esquire," a practice that began in 1962.

Under the editorship of Harold Hayes, our February 1964 issue is a good one, and indicative of where the magazine was going in the mid-1960s, with a focus on travel. Not only does the cover feature 40 stewardesses representing a number of airlines which flew to Europe, but several of the articles in our issue cover what to do and how to act after you get there. *Esquire* also released a series od "Sound Tour" albums in the mid-1960s which featured European travel advice and music.

There are three modules associated with this issue of *Esquire*. Complete any or all of them.

Module 20: The Millionaire: A Self-Portrait

This article features Wallace Johnson, the founder of the Holiday Inn hotel chain and declared "Millionaire." In it, he sprinkles advice on how to be successful, like going to college, picking the right city to start a business, eating hamburger instead of steak to save money, and the proper use of debt in building a business. How well do you think the advice in this article translates to our own time? What pieces are timeless, and which apply mostly to 1964? Why?

Module 21: Aftermath: Apocalypse at Dresden

This is a fascinating series of letters in response to a November 1963 article published in *Esquire* about the fire bombing raid on the German city of Dresden from February 13-15, 1945. Many of the letter writers fought in the European theater in World War II and their takes on the article provide a view into how the people who were in combat viewed the situation 20 years later. Which letter do you agree with most? Which is the most powerful? And if you've read Kurt Vonnegut's *Slaughterhouse Five* (which was published in 1969), how do these letters inform your understanding of the book?

Module 22: Now Voyager, a Little Attention to Ways and Means

This article is part of the travel series, and provides insight into what it was like to travel to and around Europe in 1964. There is also advice about what to wear, such as a "polo shirt, preferably faded and with a green or blue crocodile over the pocket, trademark of Rene LaCoste, the French tennis champion of the Twenties." Do you think that any of the advice presented in this article would be relevant to our time? What advice is it?

FEBRUARY 1964 · 75 CENTS

PLAYBOY

ENTERTAINMENT FOR MEN

SPECIAL JAZZ & HI-FI ISSUE

WINNERS IN PLAYBOY JAZZ POLL
THE LATEST IN HI-FI EQUIPMENT
THE PLAYBOY RECORD LIBRARY
PLAYBOY PANEL ON JAZZ TODAY
AND TOMORROW WITH STAN KENTON,
DIZZY GILLESPIE, DAVE BRUBECK,
GERRY MULLIGAN AND OTHERS
PLUS MAMIE VAN DOREN UNADORNED
BOUDOIR FUN WITH RICHARD BURTON
A NEW NOVEL BY P. G. WODEHOUSE

Playboy - February 1964

Playboy got its start when Hugh Hefener was working as a copywriter at *Esquire* and was turned down for a $5 raise. He decided to mortgage his house and raise money from family and friends (including a $1,000 loan from his mother) for a magazine that was originally going to be called *Stag Party*. The first issue of *Playboy* was released in December 1953 and featured a nude centerfold of Marilyn Monroe, taken in 1949, before she was famous. It sold 50,000 copies, and launched Hefner's publishing career.

Hefner espoused what he called "the Playboy philosophy," and it is on display in the February 1964 issue - discussions of jazz, the best stereo equipment, advice, news, famous writers, and of course, naked women. However, they're not entirely naked; just topless. In the 1960s, photography was not considered to be "pornagraphic" unless it showed pubic hair or genitals. So what changed? The publication of *Penthouse*. Started by Bob Guccione in 1965 and initially only available in Europe (due to their more broadminded attitudes about female nudity), *Penthouse* moved to the U.S. market in 1969, and began what Hugh Hefner called the "Pubic Wars." Due to the competition from *Penthouse*, *Playboy* began presenting more sexually explicit photos in 1970, and began showing pubic hair starting with the Miss January of 1971 (Liv Lindeland, who was also Playmate of the Year that year). *Hustler* began publication in 1974, and the depiction of female genitalia became far more explicit. At this point Hefner decided that *Playboy* would position itself as a "softcore" alternative which people could read for the articles.

Luckily, the articles in our February 1964 edition of *Playboy* are very good, and there are five modules associated with this edition. I've made the conscious decision NOT to include any of the centerfold pictures from the February 1964 issue (including cover model Mamie Van Doren) so that, like men of the time, we can say that we're reading *Playboy* for the articles.

Module 23: The Playboy Advisor

This is an "Ask us anything!" monthly feature of *Playboy*, and questions range from tipping croupiers at the roulette table to whether there is an aversion to green racing cars in America. Which question and answer are your favorite? What do you think about the quality of the advice? Would you provide different answers?

Module 24: The Playboy Forum

This is an "interactive" section where readers can share their ideas with the editors about "the Playboy philosophy." This was something that Hefner took seriously, even appearing on *Firing Line* in 1966, to debate William F. Buckley about its merits. Topics such as "wife swapping" (Hefner is against adultery), sophistication (Hefner is for it), and the philosophy of Immanuel Kant are featured. Which question and response are your favorite? What do you think about the quality of the letters? How do you feel the responses would be different in a mainstream magazine of our time?

Module 25: Shel Silverstein's History of *Playboy*

Silverstein was one of the most prolific cartoonists at *Playboy* from the day he was hired in 1957 through the mid-1970s. This is the second part of a three-part series on the history of *Playboy* magazine and it covers the years 1956 through 1960. What do you feel is the most interesting cartoon/story about the "Middle Years" of *Playboy*? Why?

Module 26: Men's fashion

If you'd like to know what was hip and happening in men's fashion in 1964, then look no further! Which of the looks do you believe is the most timeless or could be worn in our time? Why? And which looks the most dated?

Module 27: Party Jokes

Every issue of *Playboy* features the "Party Jokes" section, which follows the centerfold. This batch has a number of "groaners" such as "Sometimes when two's company, three's the result," but which joke is your favorite? Why?

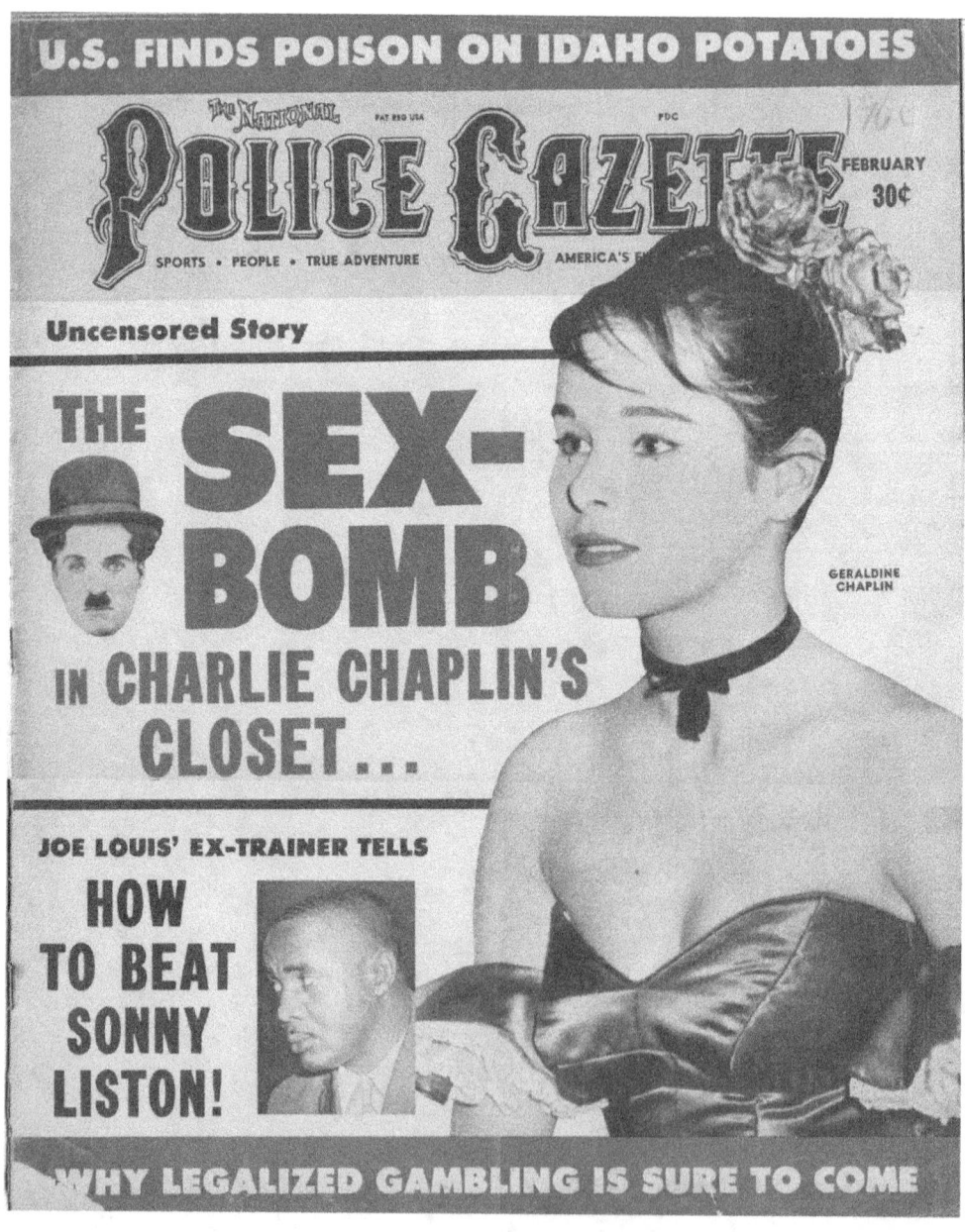

The National Police Gazette - February 1964

Imagine a magazine that combines *Playboy*, *Sports Illustrated*, *Esquire*, *National Enquirer*, and *America's Most Wanted*, and you have an idea of *Police Gazette*, a men's magazine which started publication in 1845. While it originally published crime stories in order to help police catch criminals, by the late 1800s it had become a national men's magazine which covered sports (especially boxing), celebrity gossip, and featured illustrations of burlesque dancers. It was a hit!

Our February 1964 issue covers all of the same material! And most of the article titles end in exclamation points! Complete any or all of the five modules below.

Module 28: Why I posed in the NUDE!

Mamie Van Doren is featured on the cover of the February 1964 *Playboy* and has a pictorial inside. The mystery of why she chose to pose topless in *Playboy* provides the context needed to print "cheesecake" photos of her here. With her measurements of 38-25-35, she was a hit in Hollywood, starred in movies such as *Sex Kittens Go To College* (in 1960), and was considered to be a successor to Marilyn Monroe. What do you find to be the most interesting reveal in this article about the former girlfriend of Howard Hughes?

Module 29: Beanpoles are Ruining Basketball

Wilt Chamberlain was 7'1" and dominated basketball in the 1960s, including a 100-point game on March 2, 1962. Bill Russell (also mentioned in the article) was 6"10" and excelled as a center for the Boston Celtics. Did their domination "ruin" basketball? Of course not, but reading this article in our time, the underlying point of the article seems to be that very tall, very talented African-American basketball players were changing the way the game was played. What do you think of the criticisms raised in this article? Do you feel that the same arguments could be made about basketball today? Why or why not?

Module 30: How Sonny Liston Can Be Beaten!

Sonny Liston fought Muhammad Ali (at the time known as Cassius Clay) as a 7-1 favorite on February 25, 1964. Spoiler alert! - He lost. In their rematch on May 25, 1965, Liston was knocked out in the first round. How accurate was the analysis by the reporters of *Police Gazette*? How does it compare to the analysis of Sonny Liston in *Sports Illustrated*? Since the magazine covered boxing extensively, were they more accurate in covering this sport? Why or why not?

Module 31: Legalized Gambling is Sure to Come

This article remains an amazing time capsule on sports gambling, with the prediction in 1964 of legalization in three years. It also offers insight into how "crime syndicates" have "tried to muscle in on [the] honest gamblers here in Nevada" and been "run off." Have the arguments about putting the "racketeers, dope pushers and prostitutes" out of action by legalizing sports gambling changed since 1964? Regardless, do you believe sports gambling should be legal at the national level? Why or why not?

Module 32: The Sex-Bomb in Charlie Chaplin's Closet

Spoiler alert! - It's his daughter Geraldine Chaplin. This article presents a chronicle of Charlie Chaplin's attraction to teenagers as spouses and the charges of "white slavery" brought against him. Also, he's worried about his daughter becoming an actress. For this module, research Geraldine Chaplin's acting career, as well as her father's Honorary Academy Award.

FEBRUARY 1964 · VOLUME 9 · NUMBER 6

THE HIGH SCHOOL MAGAZINE FOR HOMEMAKERS AND CAREER GIRLS · PUBLISHED BY SCHOLASTIC MAGAZINES

Single Copy, 25¢

Co-ed - February 1964

Written for female high school students, *Co-ed* was published by Scholastic from 1957 to 1985. While the cover tagline says that it is for future "homemakers and career girls," the multiple recipes, clothing ideas and advice would not be out of place on Pinterest today.

There are three modules associated with this edition of *Co-ed*. Complete any or all of them.

Module 33: Folklore and Facts

Test your knowledge of folklore and facts with this handy discussion of menstruation! Can boys tell when you're having your period by looking into your eyes? In an era before sexual education in school, do you feel that this type of article is valuable? Why or why not? And how is it different from the way the same material would be taught in our time?

Module 34: Teen Marriages

This is a nice opportunity to allow teens to weigh in on a topic that is relevant to them - teen marriage! Which is your favorite "girl" and "boy" response? How different do you think the responses would be if this question was asked today? Why?

Module 35: Advertisements

Which of the *Co-ed* advertisements is your favorite? Which most says "1964" and are there any which could be run in magazines today? Why or why not?

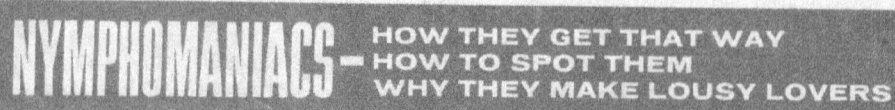

NYMPHOMANIACS — HOW THEY GET THAT WAY
HOW TO SPOT THEM
WHY THEY MAKE LOUSY LOVERS

TRUE MEN

EXTRA-LENGTH
BONUS!

STORIES   FEBRUARY   IND.

THE BEST OF BONNIE BANKS

STILL
25¢

20 YEARS AFTER THE SLAUGHTER:

WHO MURDERED EX-HITLER STORM TROOPER HANS SCHLEICHER?

(MOST INCREDIBLE SAGA OF
REVENGE TO COME OUT OF WW II)

AN INVITATION TO HIGH ADVENTURE—
"WE KNOW WHERE TO FIND THEM...
WE KNOW HOW WE'LL GET THERE . . ."

THE SEARCH GOES ON
FOR THE
LOST TREASURE
CITIES OF
EL DORADO

10 WAYS BUM COPS MAKE CRIME PAY IN YOUR OWN HOME TOWN

True Men and Guy - February 1964

If you're looking for examples of the "men's adventure" genre of magazines from the early 1960s, look no further than *True Men* and *Guy*! Known in the publishing business as "armpit slicks" or "sweats," the genre was popular throughout the 1950s and 1960s. Why?! Who would need to know about the murder of ex-Hitler Storm Trooper Hans Schlichter? Or about "The Sinful Past of Dean Martin?" Why, the readers of *True Men* and *Guy*!

There are six modules for these two magazines. Complete any or all of them.

Module 36: The Murder of ex-Hitler Storm Trooper Hans Schlichter

How can the first module not be about Hans Schlichter?! This long-form "report" about the murder of an ex-Hitler Stormtrooper (is there any other kind?) makes for compelling reading, but is any of it true? Was there an American survivor of an SS mass murder named Guido Montecarlo? Or is this just a fake story based on the Malmedy Massacre?

Module 37: Nymphomaniacs

Written by a "distinguished student of mental disorders," this article explores cases such as that of Lucille, who was expelled from college for "extending the principle of coeducation to the bedroom on an assembly line basis." It also examines subtypes of nymphomaniacs, such as the "latent lesbian," who is "fleeing from an unconscious attraction to the members of her own sex" and the "sexually vital but emotionally sterile spinster." Which subtype is your favorite? How do you think this article would be different if it had been written by a woman? Or if it was written today?

Module 38: The G.I. They Ccouldn't Kill

Audie Murphy was an undisputed hero in World War II, with a Medal of Honor and literally every award for valor (a Silver Star, two Bronze Stars, three Purple Hearts, and the list goes on) issued by the American army. This article is a somewhat sensationalized version of his story. Do you believe Audie Murphy was a product of his time or do you think that the American military still attracts such recruits? Why or why not?

Module 39: The Sinful Past of Dean Martin

Born Dino Crocetti in Steubenville in 1917, Dean Martin was a Hollywood icon by 1964. While this article promises to inform the reader about his "sinful" past, it's difficult to ascertain what he did that was particularly immoral. His prizefighting career? Growing up in the 1920s? What revelations in this article did you find surprising?

Module 40: New York Jungle

When FBI Chief J. Edgar Hoover testifies to a "terrifying pace of youthful lawlessness," *Guy* magazine is there with an article about Bat Man and his accomplice Big. While the article reads like the unshot scenes from *West Side Story*, it brings up ideas about the juvenile delinquency occurring in America at the time. In what ways do you believe that juvenile crime has changed? What are the solutions from our time that can be applied to the youth of 1964?

Module 41: Advertisements

The readers of *True Men* and *Guy* magazine have very specific ads aimed at them. Which ads do you think are most effective? Why? Would any still work in our time?

Mad magazine - January and March 1964

Soon after *Mad* magazine began publishing in 1952, a reader wrote in, "What you publish is cheap, miserable trash. Fortunately, I also am cheap, miserable trash!" Thus was the tone set for the multi-decade run of a magazine written by "the usual gang of idiots."

Mad began in a comic book format before switching to a magazine in 1955. The reason? Censorship. In the early 1950's Fredric Werthham wrote about the destructiveness of comic books on the minds of children in his book *Seduction of the Innocent*. Comics publishers switched to self-censorship of their material, but by changing the dimensions of the product (from comic book to magazine), *Mad* was able to become a satire magazine and dodge the censorship. Since *Mad* carried no interior advertising from 1957 until 2001, there were no advertisers to offend, and so the writers were unhindered and able to produce the work they wanted and loved. They also created their OWN advertisements (see the module below).

The switch from comic book to magazine also brought mascot Alfred E. Neuman to the cover of almost every issue. Originally modeled after a face used in early 20th century ads for "painless dentistry," the Neuman mascot was conceived as a "visual logo" in the same way as the Jolly Green Giant. His motto of "What, me worry?" was derived from the same "painless dentistry" ads, which I think makes it even funnier.

Mad was not published monthly, but rather eight times a year, with double issues for Jan/Feb, March/April, July/Aug, and Oct/Nov. Another interesting anomaly was that issues would come out up to two months before the date on the magazine, so that the December issue would come out in October. It's mad! And is why I'm including both the January and March 1964 issues in this book - both were available in February 1964.

The January 1964 cover features a "Christmas seal" (groan) and the March cover is a play on Lincoln's birthday (February 12th). There are five modules associated with these issues of *Mad*. Complete any or all of them.

Module 42: Celebrities' Nightmares

Proof that *Mad* came out two months before the date on the magazine is obvious from this pictorial, which features President Kennedy dreaming about British model Christine Keeler (the instigator of the Profumo scandal). Which cartoon is your favorite? Why?

Module 43: Modern Teacher magazine

Being a teacher has always had its difficulties, and *Mad* magazine is happy to bring them up. My favorite is the "Simon Pure Books," which are rewrites of "subversive" books. Which article is your favorite? And has anything changed in teaching since 1964?

Module 44: The Lighter Side of . . . The College Crowd

Animal House was still 14 years in the future, but David Berg's "The Lighter Side of . . . " feature attempts to capture college life in 1964. How is it the same and different as college life today, or if you went to college, how it was for you?

Module 45: When They Use Numbers for Everything

While this isn't "laugh out loud" funny, it reflects the zeitgeist of 1964's infatuation with numbers and privacy (see *The Ed Sullivan Show* and *The Atlantic*). In our era of "big data," does this feature seem outdated or prescient? Why or why not?

Module 46: Advertisements

This is my favorite feature in *Mad* magazine of this time. Which is your favorite ad? Why? Do you think that any could be worked into ads for our time?

A JOHNSON PUBLICATION

EBONY

NEGROES WHO FOUGHT ON BUNKER HILL

HOW JFK SURPASSED ABRAHAM LINCOLN

SMOOTH SAILING
In Newest Swimsuits

FEBRUARY 1964 50c

Ebony - February 1964

The first issue of *Ebony* appeared on November 1, 1945 with a print run of 25,000 copies. It sold out quickly, and publisher John H. Johnson knew that he had a hit. His wife Eunice had come up with the name for the magazine, and the intention was to create a version of *Life* for America's African-American community.

By the mid-1960s, Ebony was covering the civil rights movement, and there's a module about the first African-American registered to vote in a Louisiana parish in 61 years. I'll write that again - 61 YEARS. It's incredible to me that this was once what parts of America were like.

This month's cover features model Janie Burdette, who was something of a "regular" in *Ebony*, usually modeling the latest fashions. Based on the West Coast, this is the first time she was featured on the cover. The photographer, Christa, described her as an excellent model . . . she can model everything from swim suits to high fashion formal gowns."

Ebony and *Jet* were both eventually sold to a private equity firm with the death of publisher John H. Johnson, and *Ebony* is now available only in digital issues.

There are three modules associated with this edition of *Ebony*. Complete any or all of them.

Module 47: Birth of a Voter

This is a fascinating article about Rev. Joseph Carter and his wife Wilmeda, as he was going to register to vote after being arrested for trying to register to vote the previous year. He was held in police custody for 13 hours. The chronicle of the courage it took to undertake this simple registration is riveting. What are your thoughts about this article and the time it portrays? How have things changed in America, and what parallels do you see to our own time?

Module 48: Three-State Vice President

This article is about Yolande H. Chambers and her work with the 5,000 employees of a 51-store department store chain. While her experience was extraordinary in 1964, do you feel it would be so today? Why or why not?

Module 49: Advertisements

The advertisements in *Ebony* are reflective of their time. To what extent to do feel that they reflect African-American culture of the time? Are they just the same mainstream ads with African-American models, or are they different from other advertising of the time? And which ads do you think could still run today?

20c

JET

WILL ATLANTA BECOME ANOTHER BIRMINGHAM?

FEB. 6, 1964

CARL T. ROWAN

CARL T. ROWAN:
Former Ambassador to
Finland and prize-
winning journalist
succeeds the famed
Edward R. Murrow

New Chief
Of America's
Info Agency

PRESIDENT
LYNDON B. JOHNSON

STEPHEN E.
SMITH

Jet - February 6, 1964

The first issue of *Jet* appeared in 1951 with the intention of providing news about African-American culture and entertainment. Publisher John H. Johnson had started the monthly magazine *Ebony* in 1945, and based on its success, believed that there was a market for a weekly digest of stories too. The name *Jet* was thought to symbolize "Black and speed" according to Johnson.

Jet became a chronicle of the Civil Rights movement throughout the 1950s, and rose to national prominence when it published photos of the mutilated body of Emmett Till, a 14-year-old who was lynched in Mississippi after being accused of offending a white woman in her family's grocery store. His murderers were acquitted by an all-white jury in 1955. Since they didn't have to fear prosecution due to double jeopardy (where a person can't be tried twice for the same crime), Till's assailants admitted to the murder in an interview with *Look* magazine in 1956.

This week's cover features President Johnson and Carl T. Rowan, the former ambassador to Finland and the newly appointed chief of the United States Information Agency (USIA) and the subject of the first module. There are six modules associated with this edition of *Jet*. Complete any or all of them.

Module 50: Carl T. Rowan

Carl T. Rowan was a highly respected journalist when he was appointed an Assistant Secretary of State by President Kennedy, and then ambassador to Finland in 1962. President Johnson appointed him to head the USIA, which also gave him a seat on the National Security Council. While this story is also covered in the February 3rd *Newsweek*, how do you feel that the coverage is different in *Jet*? Why?

Module 51: Two-Gun Pete

"Twenty years I was a policeman. Now my own woman lets me have it." So says Sylvester Washington, famous as a Chicago policeman known as "Two-Gun Pete." I've included a *Chicago Tribune* video about this famous lawman to see how things turned out for him. In the end, what is your opinion of Two-Gun Pete? Do we need officers like him today? Or do you think that he was more a product of his time? Why?

Module 53: Ray Charles

Described by his girlfriend Sandra Jean Betts as a "master of words," this paternity suit cost Ray Charles $125,000 (about a million dollars inflation-adjusted). However, her description of Ray Charles (especially his love of television) is interesting to read. How do you think Ray Charles comes across in this article? Does it change your opinion of him? Why or why not?

Module 54: People Are Talking About

This is one of the most entertaining features of *Jet* - short and gossipy blurbs of news. My personal favorite is the names that arrested sit-in students gave to the police. Which is your favorite? Why?

Module 55: Muhammad Ali

While he was still known as Cassius Clay in 1964, this is a fascinating article about Muhammad Ali attending a dinner with Malcolm X. It even includes a poem! What do you think about his ideas on integration? How are they similar and different from views on the subject today?

Module 56: Rats to Rockefeller

This is an interesting article about community action on the subject of rat eradication! How do you think activists would handle a situation like this today?

USSR

FEBRUARY 1964
25 Cents

SOVIET LIFE TODAY

USSR: Soviet Life Today - February 1964

In 1956, the United States and Soviet Union agreed to begin a magazine exchange in order to improve cross-cultural understanding between their citizens. The Soviet Union got *Amerika*, and we got *USSR - Soviet Life Today*. Both were what was known as "polite propaganda" and featured stories about daily life in each respective country. While *Amerika* featured articles such as "Best Dressed College Girls" and the material riches of the United States (televisions, supermarkets, and cars), *Soviet Life* was more about Marxism as an ideology and the life of workers in the "workers' paradise" of the Soviet Union. Approximately 30,000 copies of each magazine were distributed each month until the Soviet Union was dissolved in December 1991. The September 1991 cover of Soviet Life featured Boris Yeltsin waving a Russian Federation flag with the tagline of "People Choose Democracy," so the magazine wasn't going to last past the end of the Soviet Union.

However, the February 1964 issue of *USSR - Soviet Life Today* is a good one! There are four modules associated with this issue. Complete any or all of them!

Module 57: Is Marxism Outdated?

Spoiler alert: It isn't - at least according to this article by philosopher Fyodor Konstantinov. He argues that socialism works(!) and that the Soviet Union is a model for the rest of the world. Knowing how things turned out for the Soviet Union, why do you think people believed in the Soviet system? Are the future failures evident in an article from 1964? Why or why not?

Module 58: A Citizen is Born

Ostensibly this is an article about children, but the subtext reads very differently. Did you know that the average lifespan in the Soviet Union is 70 years (it was actually 67 in 1964 - it is 73 today)? Or that 100% of the national income of the USSR goes to 100% of the people? The children featured in this article would be in their 50s and 60s today. Think about all of the changes they witnessed in their society over their lifetime. What has occurred for the better? What is worse?

Module 59: Reader Questions

How many books are published in the Soviet Union every year? Just one of the many questions asked by American readers of *USSR - Soviet Life Today* and answered in this column! What question would you want (truthfully) answered if you wrote to the magazine in 1964?

Module 60: Young Workers Today

Each of the "young workers" gets to tell a little about themselves and their aspirations. Who is your favorite? Why?

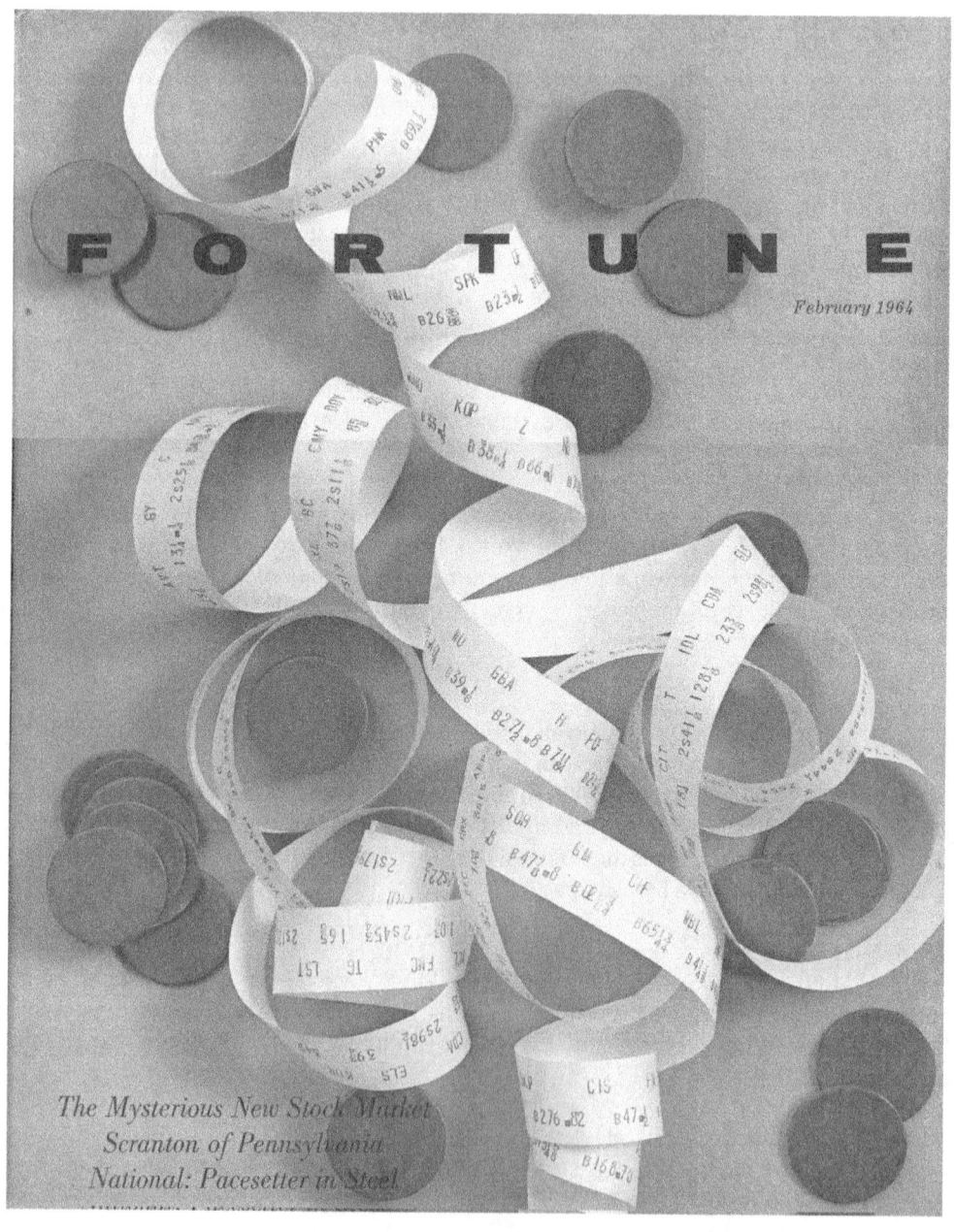

FORTUNE

February 1964

The Mysterious New Stock Market
Scranton of Pennsylvania
National: Pacesetter in Steel

Fortune - February 1964

Henry Luce, the founder of *Time* magazine in 1923, decided in 1929 that there needed to be a business magazine "vividly portraying, interpreting, and recording the Industrial Civilization." But what about the Crash of 1929? Luce had an answer for that too: "We will not be over-optimistic. We will recognize that this business slump may last as long as an entire year." And with that, the inaugural issue of *Fortune* came out in February 1930 with a price of $1 per copy, or an inflation-adjusted $15.77! Why would someone pay so much for a business publication during the Depression? Because they already had 30,000 subscribers for the first issue! It's amazing to me that by 1937 - the literal depths of the Depression - Fortune had 460,000 subscribers and was making a profit of half a million dollars per year.

Our February 1964 copy of *Fortune* sold for $1.25, or an inflation-adjusted $10.60 - since I bought it on ebay for $15, it appears that it's value has held up pretty well! The magazine was intended to be high-end and beautiful, and it is. It's oversized at 11"x 14" and is printed on heavy paper, with color photographs throughout. If you were wealthy in 1964, then this was your business magazine.

There are four modules associated with this issue of *Fortune*. Complete any or all of them.

Module 61: New Forces in the Stock Market

Out of a 1964 population of 191 million, 17 million Americans (or 9% of the population) owned shares in the stock market. In our time, it's closer to 55%, with the peak of 67% in 2002. But the stock market was very different in 1964. Or was it? After all, this article discusses the choices of individual investors and the benefits of "dollar-cost averaging!" Compare and contrast the average investor of today to the average investor in 1964. How are they the same and different? Why?

Module 62: The Science of Being Almost Certain

Statistics, and their application to decision-making, was a new concept in 1964. This article provides a "college-education level" explanation of Bayesian statistical methods in making predictions, and it's pretty fascinating to see a science in its infancy. In what ways do you feel that our world is now dominated by statistics? What are the good and bad ramifications?

Module 63: We're Losing the Supersonic Transport Race

The Anglo-French development of the Concorde made the American aerospace industry very nervous in 1964. To paraphrase the film *Dr. Strangelove* (which premiered on January 29, 1964), people were worried about a "supersonic transport gap!" But the American aerospace industry never built a commercial SST. How did that decision turn out? For this module, research the history of the Concorde and the pros and cons of developing a commercial supersonic transport.

Module 64: Advertising to America's corporate elite

The full-page color advertisements in Fortune are amazing, and works of art in their own right. Which is your favorite? Which ads could still be run today? Why?

February 1964, 75 cents

THE Atlantic

THE GHASTLY BLANK

by ALAN MOOREHEAD

The
First
Exploration
of
Australia

also

MARTHA GELLHORN
ARCHIBALD MacLEISH
SAMUEL ELIOT MORISON

The Atlantic - February 1964

First published as *The Atlantic Monthly* in 1857, editor James Russell Lowell was able to attract the preeminent writers of the day (Ralph Waldo Emerson, Henry Wadsworth Longfellow, Harriet Beecher Stow, etc.) to write on topics such as political issues, education, and the abolition of slavery. Since it was published in Boston, it retained a "New England" reputation, even after it achieved national circulation.

Unlike its later competitor *The New Yorker*, which was created to appeal to an urban (and urbane) readership, *The Atlantic* has always been more of a general interest magazine, and this remains true for our February 1964 issue, which covers issues from geopolitics to privacy in American culture.

There are four modules associated with this edition of *The Atlantic*. Complete any or all of them.

Module 65: Report on Washington

This is an interesting article for the context that it provides for the international political situation in February 1964. De Gaulle had recently recognized Communist China, and there was concern about the stability of America's NATO allies. Was this analysis prescient for how things would progress? Why or why not?

Module 66: A eulogy for JFK

Harvard history professor Samuel Eliot Morison was charged by *The Atlantic* to write a eulogy examining JFK's place in history. How accurate was he? How is President Kennedy viewed differently in our time versus February 1964? Why do you believe that is?

Module 67: The Invasion of Privacy

"Are there forces now loose in our world that threaten to annihilate everybody's privacy?" So asks this essay by Vance Packard. In 1964! It's interesting that the article is concerned with the proliferation of surveillance cameras, which have become ubiquitous in large cities in our time. Do you feel that privacy is more of an issue in our time than in 1964? Or is this always an issue in different times and in different ways?

Module 68: How to Outwit Forms

The Committee for the Abolition of Unprofitable Paperwork is trying to limit the spread of redundant forms in large organizations. How is this the same and different in terms of the ubiquity of email in the workplace in our time? Would the solutions from 1964 work in our own time? Why or why not?

FEBRUARY 1964   35 CENTS ICD

SCIENCE DIGEST

'I EXPECT TO CATCH HELL'

A KINSEY COLLEAGUE REPORTS ON MARRIAGE AS IT REALLY IS

WINTER HEALTH—SHOULD YOU GO SOUTH?
MEET OUR FIRST WOMAN NOBEL PRIZE WINNER
SST: AVIATION'S BIG LEAP IN THE DARK

Science Digest - February 1964

Published from 1937 through 1988 by the Hearst Corporation, *Science Digest* was aimed at educated people looking for monthly updates on progress in science and technology. Many of the articles (including those from the February 1964 issue) are excerpted from longer articles in other publications in the manner of *Reader's Digest*. If you equate science with the pursuit of the "truth," then these articles make for fascinating reading!

There are four modules for this edition of *Science Digest*. Complete any or all of them!

Module 69: Marriage as it really is

"For many couples, sex becomes a predictable, brief, Saturday night encounter in which the parties concerned are anesthetized by alcohol." Talk about romance! Are the findings of Dr. Cuber congruent with your experience of relationships? And what do you think about his conclusions? After reading this article, how do you think marriage in 1964 differed from today? Was it better, worse, or about the same? Why?

Module 70: Aviation's leap in the dark

With an article in this month's *Fortune* too, the idea of a supersonic jet was very much on the minds of people in early 1964. The *Science Digest* article goes in a very different direction though, with fears of radiation levels impacting pregnant female passengers and questions about the commercial viability of an SST. The article predicts 125 Concordes in operation by the mid-1970s - research how many were actually in operation! Also, why do you believe the Concorde was a failure?

Module 71: The poet is a computer

What will computers be able to do next?! As someone who teaches classes in cognitive science, I have to ask whether the RCA 301 computer is actually writing poetry or whether Clair Phillippy is just pressing a button and recording the word that is chosen. For this module, research the present state of "machine-generated" poetry, as well as the DeepMind project, which harnesses AI to create novel solutions to problems.

Module 72: Columbus wasn't first!

Is it possible to "discover" a continent where people are already living? Putting that aside, the archeological study of Norse settlements in North America was cutting-edge in 1964. For this module, research the current status of the theory that Erik the Red (and others) discovered and settled the New World. What do you think about the validity of this theory? Why?

Universal International News - February 3, 1964

The *Universal International News* newsreels were released every week by Universal Studios from 1929 to 1967. They were always shot in black and white (even after color film became available) and were shown in theaters before movies! However, with the advent of widely available television news, the days of newsreels were numbered.

Another interesting fact about the *Universal International News* newsreels is that in 1974 the entire collection was donated to the National Archives and placed into the "public domain." This means that anyone can use them without attribution or royalties - one of the reasons why the footage ends up in so many documentaries and history shows!

There are three modules associated with this newsreel. Complete any or all of them.

Module 73: Ranger 6

"A 28 million dollar trip of 230,000 miles" is the synopsis of the Ranger 6 launch to the moon. Except that it was a bust, and failed to take any pictures of the lunar surface - it's primary mission. Why do you think that a failed rocket mission is the first story in the newsreel? Why was the public so interested in space travel in 1964?

Module 74: Men's Favorite Sport

Paula Prentiss had a busy early 1960s, starring in *Where the Boys Are* in 1960, marrying actor Richard Benjamin in 1961, and starring with Rock Hudson in 1963's *Man's Favorite Sport*. How is this newsworthy? Or is the goal to show the beauty contest winners? Or promote a Universal film? Or all of the above? Regardless, how have movie premieres and marketing changed since 1964?

Module 75: Winter Olympics!

Rudolph Itkovitch is able to speak ten different languages - which is nine more than most of us! What do you think of the focus of the newsreel? Does highlighting husband/wife Russian skaters and French sibling skiers speak to an audience from 1964 differently than an audience from our time? How do you feel that the coverage of the athletes is different in 1964 than today?

The Beatles Arrive in New York - February 7, 1964

Documentary filmmaker Albert Maysles received a phone call from Grenada Television two hours before the Beatles landed in New York, asking if he and his brother David would be interested in making a film about them. Albert agreed, and then turned to his brother and said, "Who are the Beatles? Are they any good?"

They rushed to the airport, and the footage they shot is invaluable. It was released in 1964 as *What's Happening! The Beatles in the U.S.A.* and there are four modules associated with this media. Complete any or all of them.

Module 76: The Press Conference

Upon landing, the Beatles held a press conference where they were asked about their hair, their popularity, and a number of other things. Their confidence, poise, and wit is on display. Which answer do you think is best or funniest? Why?

Module 77: The Ride to the Hotel

This is my absolute favorite footage of the day, and I even purchased a Pepsi transistor radio like the one Paul listens to! What are your impressions of the Beatles upon their arrival at the hotel? Would you be thrilled or frightened by the presence of so many screaming fans? Why?

Module 78: In the Hotel Room

This is intimate footage of the Beatles in their hotel room, taking calls from Murray the K and watching television. What is your favorite moment in this footage? Why?

THIRTY CENTS

FEBRUARY 7, 1964

TIME

THE WEEKLY NEWSMAGAZINE

THE SIREN'S SONG
French Diplomacy from Richelieu to De Gaulle

FOREIGN MINISTER
COUVE DE MURVILLE

VOL. 83 NO. 6
(REG. U.S. PAT. OFF.)

Time - February 7, 1964

The original goal of Briton Hadden and Henry Luce (the founders of *Time*) was to create a weekly newsmagazine that could be read in an hour. The idea was to report the news through a focus on people, which is why for decades the cover of *Time* featured a single person - in the February 7th edition, French foreign minister Maurice Couve de Murville, who held the post from 1958 to 1968, when he became Prime Minister. However, other magazines cover the French political moves of early 1964 better, so there are no modules associated with him for this issue. As an aside, *Time* was originally going to be called *Facts*. There's a joke there somewhere! There are four modules associated with this edition of *Time*. Complete any or all of them.

Module 79: Racial Unrest in Atlanta and Cross-Bussing

I decided to combine these two articles into one module because I believe they indicate the battles of the Civil Rights movement in both the American South (demonstrations in Atlanta) and the North (school boycotts in New York). Rabbi Myron Fenster is quoted as saying "If the whole society is rotten, why start with me? I don't want to take the first step. I want to take the last step." Compare and contrast school segregation and solutions from 1964 and today. What do you believe is the best way to make progress in creating equal opportunity in education?

Module 80: Poverty and Passion

Michael Harrington's book *The Other America: Poverty in the U.S.* became a prime inspiration for Lyndon Johnson's Great Society programs. A democratic socialist, Harrington advocated for a "passion to end poverty" to create a more equal America. How do you believe his ideas are the same and different from the proposals of today? Do you believe his ideas would work better or worse in our own time?

Module 81: The Space Program

You have to have a real interest in the space program to enjoy this module, but it celebrates the success of both the Ranger 6 moon probe (which is also in the Universal newsreel) and the successful launch of the first Saturn 5 rocket - the rocket that would take us to the moon! Research the rocket scientist mentioned in the article, Dr. Wernher von Braun, on his controversial past and contributions to the space program. In this case, do the ends justify the means?

Module 82: Beyond the Transistor

Who knows? The revolution in microcircuitry "may eventually lead to the long-heralded TV set that hangs on the wall like a picture." Can anyone imagine a future like that?! This article makes clear that the computer industry was at a crossroads in 1964, with the use of vacuum tubes, transistors, and "microcircuits" all contributing to progress. But that was 60 years ago. If you were writing such an article today, what advances and consumer products would you predict to be in production 60 years from now? Maybe "Dick Tracy's two-way wrist radio?"

74

LIFE

TANGANYIKA:
BRITISH COMMANDO BRINGS
IN CAPTURED MUTINEERS

FEBRUARY 7 · 1964 · 25¢

Life - February 7, 1964

Although it started as a successful humor magazine in 1883 with the motto "Where there's life, there's hope," it was bought in 1936 by *Time* publisher Henry Luce for $92,000 just for the name. Literally. He sold the subscription list and content to the rival humor magazine *Judge*. Luce believed that what the market needed was a new large format magazine which told stories primarily through pictures. And that was *Life* magazine. The motto was changed to "To see *Life*; to see the world."

By the early 1960s the magazine was full of color pictures of politicians (primarily members of the Kennedy family) and movie stars. For example, later in 1964 *Life* ran a 6,000 word article on the relationship between Elizabeth Taylor and Richard Burton, with pictures of them in Hollywood, New York, and Paris.

Our February 7th 1964 issue isn't quite so glitzy, with the cover featuring a British commando with prisoners in Tanganyika (which became the nation of Tanzania). While there are still plenty of pictures of politicians (primarily Barry Goldwater, Nelson Rockefeller, and Richard Nixon, posing with his dog Checkers), they still manage to work JFK in, with a pictorial on models of the future Kennedy Center for the Performing Arts. However, the three modules associated with this issue will cover other news.

Module 83: Marilyn's Ghost Takes the Stage

While it wasn't in the same league as *Death of a Salesman* or *The Crucible*, Arthur Miller's "new" play about his deceased second wife, Marilyn Monroe, played by his soon-to-be third wife, Barbara Loden, was considered by many to be in bad taste. In fact, Jackie Kennedy, who had been a friend to Miller, cut off contact with him over his depiction of Marilyn Monroe in the play - she saw it as disloyalty to a departed loved one. After reading Arthur Miller's defense of the play in *Life*, do you feel that it deserves to be one of his least popular works? Why or why not?

Module 84: The Fearmongers

This is a contemporaneous story about what racist hate groups were up to in 1964, and can be difficult to read for someone from our time. How do you think things have changed in America in terms of race from 1964 to our time? How were the efforts of the people in this article overcome?

Module 85: Why Does a Man Become a Hater?

While psychoanalyst Bruno Bettleheim had an international reputation in the 1960s, and was approached by *Life* to do this article, after his death he has been plagued by accusations that he faked most of his academic credentials, and was not only *not* certified in psychoanalysis, but had only ever taken three classes in psychology. His plagiarism has also become legendary. Putting that aside, what do you think of his analysis of Lee Harvey Oswald and hate groups? What about his ideas for dealing with extremism?

The New Yorker - February 8, 1964

The New Yorker has always prided itself on journalistic sophistication, with founder Harold Ross declaring that it is "not edited for the old lady in Dubuque." And he would know, because he edited the weekly magazine from the inaugural issue of February 21, 1925 until his death in 1951. For our 1964 issue, *The New Yorker* was edited by William Shawn, who held the position from 1951 through his retirement in 1987. So there hasn't been much turnover at *The New Yorker*, and in terms of cover artwork, typography, and interior layout, changes have been minimal.

Besides being known for long-form journalism and short stories, *The New Yorker* is known for single-panel cartoons. The cartoons are often very clever and have sometimes started catch phrases, most famously in 1941, where a man walking away from his crashed plane announces, 'Well, back to the old drawing board."

Our February 8, 1964 edition features cover art of birds over a rural scene of a woman filling a bird feeder by illustrator Art Birnbaum. He painted over 200 covers for *The New Yorker* surrounded by his 15 cats, and was known for painting people and animals "in their most uncomplicated terms." According to his obituary in *The New York Times,* "he would draw an object such as a chair 200 times or more to get it right." He passed away in 1966.

There are three modules associated with this edition of *The New Yorker.* Complete any or all of them.

Module 86: The cartoons
   Which of the cartoons in this issue do you think is the funniest? Why? Which one most says "1964" to you?

Module 87: The advertisements
   It's not just the writing that's sophisticated in *The New Yorker*, but the ads too! Which ad is your favorite, and why? Which ads do you think worked better in 1964 than today? What do these ads say about the typical reader of *The New Yorker*?

Module 88: The Honored Society
   The long-form articles in *The New Yorker* are long, so I wanted to limit them to just one for these modules. This "Profiles" piece is about the Mafia in Sicily as the Americans encountered it in 1943 during World War II. The article is fascinating because it explores how while it exists outside of Catholic morality, the Mafia "has an iron morality of its own." Vendettas from the 1870s are explored and explained. It's interesting because the article goes into detail about the city of Corleone, yet precedes *The Godfather* films by nearly a decade. What do you think of their portrayal of the Mafia in this article? Is Don Calo an understandable and/or sympathetic character? Why or why not?

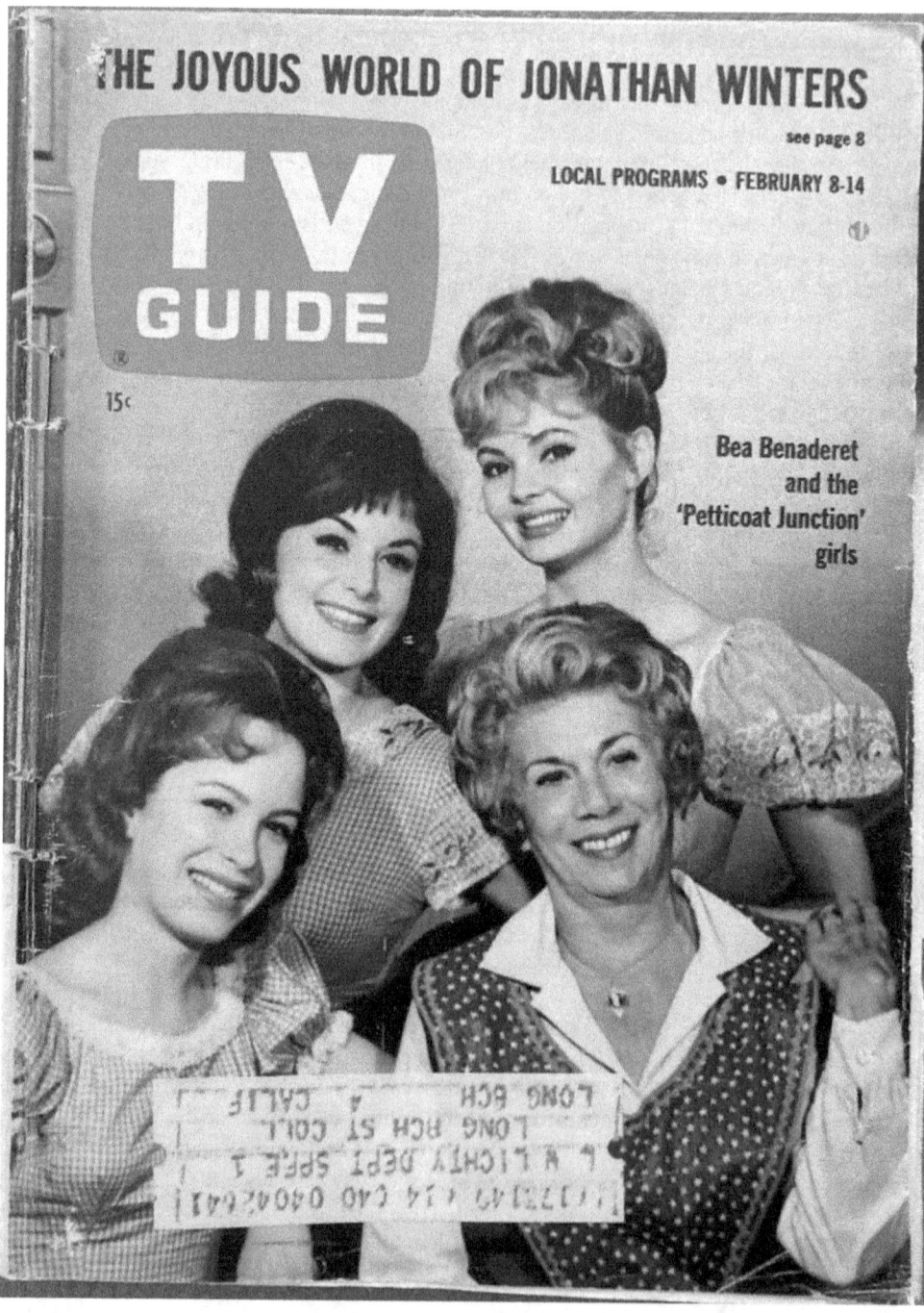

THE JOYOUS WORLD OF JONATHAN WINTERS

see page 8

LOCAL PROGRAMS • FEBRUARY 8-14

TV GUIDE

15¢

Bea Benaderet
and the
'Petticoat Junction'
girls

The Day

This second section is dedicated to the events of one day - February 9th 1964. There is a mix of print and visual media, and it is presented chronologically throughout the day, so the day begins with the delivery of *The New York Times* and ends with *What's My Line?* (which aired at 1030PM - I go to bed early). How do I know what was on television on February 9th 1964? *TV Guide*! It allows us to know what specific episodes of television shows were on that day, and at what time.

The morning is represented by the arrival of three newspapers, *The New York Times* and *The New York Times Magazine*, and the *National Enquirer*.

Since I like to have music on at lunch, the top five songs for the week will be presented at that "time."

Late afternoon and early evening features reruns of *Maverick* (at noon and 6PM), and *The Adventures of Robin Hood* (on at 4PM), along with the animated *Return to Oz* (at 5PM).

Prime time television is part of the day too, beginning with *The Adventures of Ozzie and Harriet*, *My Favorite Martian*, and *The Wonderful World of Disney's Scarecrow of Romney Marsh*. We then move on to the "prime" prime time shows of *The Ed Sullivan Show* (Featuring the Beatles!), the *Judy Garland Show*, and *Bonanza*.

The Day ends with *What's My Line?*, with guests Bobby Darin and Jane Fonda. However, I've also included a short clip of the Beatles dancing out at a club after *The Ed Sullivan Show*. They were having a great time on their first night in New York City!

Thus, The Day begins and ends in New York City, where *The New York Times* is published, where the Beatles performed, where *What's My Line?* was shot, and where the Beatles were partying.

The New York Times.

"All the News That's Fit to Print"

NEWS SUMMARY AND INDEX, PAGE 91

LATE CITY EDITION

Partly cloudy and cold today; clear tonight. Fair and cold tomorrow.
Temp. Range: 36—23; yesterday: 39—29.

SECTION ONE

VOL. CXIII. No. 38,732.

NEW YORK, SUNDAY, FEBRUARY 9, 1964.

THIRTY CENTS

JOBS-ISSUE BLOCKS ATTEMPT IN HOUSE TO VOTE ON RIGHTS

Southern Motions to Amend Bill Force a Delay, With New Debate Tomorrow

REPUBLICANS ARE ANGRY

But Halleck Fails to Prevent an Adjournment — Final Action Due Tuesday

By E. W. KENWORTHY
Special to The New York Times

WASHINGTON, Feb. 8—The House failed to complete action on the civil rights bill tonight after logging down in a morass of amendments to the section outlawing discrimination by employers and labor unions.

At 10:13 P.M. the House adjourned until 11 A.M. Monday when it will resume debate on one of the most controversial sections in the omnibus bill.

The chances for a final vote Monday on the whole bill are probably slim. However, a final vote must be taken by Tuesday.

On the question of adjournment, the Northern bipartisan coalition broke ranks for the first time.

G.O.P. Wants to Stay

The Republicans wanted to stay all night, if necessary, so that they could get away for the traditional Lincoln's Birthday speech-making.

They were resentful when Representative Emanuel Celler, Democrat of Brooklyn, who is floor manager for the bill, put the motion to adjourn.

As the Northern Democrats stood up in support of Mr. Celler, loyal cries of "Coalition! Coalition!" arose from the Republican ranks.

The Republicans under Charles A. Halleck of Indiana, were so angry that he demanded a roll-call on adjournment, a most unusual request. The motion to adjourn carried, 220 to 175.

Fate Never in Doubt

However, with the Southerners showing no signs of running out of amendments, it was doubtful that action on the key employment section and the close remaining sections could have been completed by dawn.

It was a tumultuous day. The final fate of the section was never in doubt, as two demonstrated tonight when a coalition to kill it entirely was easily defeated, 180 to 90.

Nevertheless, the civil rights supporters were forced to accede to some unexpected amendments, including one to include sex among the prohibited reasons for refusing employment along with race, color, religion and national origin. Another amendment would allow an employer to refuse to hire an atheist.

The Southerners were in no mood to hurry the proceedings in so-orthodoxize the Northern coalition, and they felt as
Continued on Page 52, Column 1

Donovan Assigned Bodyguard as Mail Threatens His Life

By GENE CURRIVAN

A police bodyguard has been assigned to James B. Donovan, president of the Board of Education, as a result of threatening letters he received from integration extremists.

This was acknowledged by Mr. Donovan yesterday when he was pressed to explain the presence of an "aide" who is with him most of the time. Mr. Donovan said the man he had introduced as a board aide was actually a plainclothes policeman, who has assigned to him all these days.

The board president said he had received many letters threatening his life. He added, moreover, that of the "thousands of letters" he had received in the present dispute over the board's plans for fuller integration of city schools, the ratio had been "a toss-up," one in its my favor.

Meanwhile, dissatisfied civil rights groups that conducted a boycott of the schools last
Continued on Page 57, Column 6

STATES AID URGED FOR THE ELDERLY

President Praises Cabinet Study Seeking Job-Bias Ban and Housing Aid

By TOM WICKER
Special to The New York Times

AUSTIN, Tex., Feb. 8—A Cabinet-level Council on Aging reported to President Johnson today on the need for state laws to prevent discrimination against elderly persons.

The council also suggested private programs to permit older persons to "taper off" in their jobs, rather than be forced to retire at a specified time. A number of other recommendations were made in the fields of employment, housing and welfare services.

Mr. Johnson received the report at the LBJ Ranch, where he was spending the weekend and adding to it an urgent call for "the enactment of hospital insurance for the aged through Social Security to help older people meet the high costs of illness without jeopardizing their economic independence."

Asks State Action

"This program would not only be a major attack on health problems among older people but a major attack on poverty," he said.

At the same time, Mr. Johnson said, the states should "adopt adequate programs of medical assistance for the aged under the Kerr-Mills legislation."

"This assistance is needed now and it will be needed later in certain states as a supplement to hospital insurance to deal with those special problems that private insurance and social costs present," he said.

Mr. Johnson urged humane and industry to give careful consideration to the recommendations of the Council on Aging. He said an Administration had requested $19 billion in housing and trust funds "for benefits and services for older persons."
Continued on Page 55, Column 1

Police Are Picketed Over Slum Eviction

By RICHARD STENGREN

The next strike was carried to Police Headquarters yesterday by pickets charging the charge that "police protect slumlords."

They demanded the dismissal of a policeman who on Friday arrested the leader of the pickets tenant movement.

A letter went out to the Grove Street as the shouts of 75 pickets echoed between the closed shops of heavy-machinery dealers and the fortress-like Police headquarters building.

The demonstration was the latest phase of a movement that began last November against slum landlords whose buildings are inhabited with rats and were run-down in which there are tenants with thick with overcrowding.

HOME DENOUNCES 'OFFENSIVE' NOTE FROM KHRUSHCHEV

Tells Him Sharply That Views on Cyprus Are Unfounded — Ball Sent to London

By LAWRENCE FELLOWS
Special to The New York Times

LONDON, Feb. 8 — Prime Minister Sir Alec Douglas-Home accused Premier Khrushchev tonight of making offensive and unfounded charges about Britain's attempts to keep the peace in Cyprus.

In his reply to a message received from the Soviet Premier yesterday, Sir Alec suggested to Mr. Khrushchev not only that he was in error, but also that he was contributing to the high level of passions in that island republic and making the situation more difficult.

[Under Secretary of State George W. Ball was ordered to London to join the negotiations over a peace-keeping force on Cyprus.]

Mr. Khrushchev, in message to Sir Alec, President Johnson, President de Gaulle, Premier Inonu of Turkey, Premier John Paraskevopoulos of Greece and President Makarios of Cyprus, condemned what he called a plan by allied leaders to organize "military intervention" in Cyprus.

Soviet Asserts an Interest

The Soviet Premier said that because the Eastern Mediterranean was not so far removed from the southern Soviet Union, his Government could not remain indifferent to the situation in Cyprus.

In his reply tonight Sir Alec said: "I will not conceal from you that I have been surprised and disappointed to receive the message which you sent me on Feb. 7 about the situation in Cyprus.

"I am surprised," Sir Alec continued, "that the Soviet Government should have formed a view of this question which is completely divorced from reality and I am disappointed that, on the basis of that view, you have seen fit to make charges which are as offensive as they are unfounded."

1,700 Troops on Island

Britain, at the invitation of the leaders of the embattled Cypriote communities, has committed about 2,700 combat troops to patrolling the island and to manning a thin tension zone in Nicosia since early March for the large Christmas week.

With the situation in Cyprus beginning to deteriorate, with the danger of Greece and Turkey being drawn into the conflict in support of the fighting communities on the island, Britain has sought to engage the United States and other members of the North Atlantic Treaty Organization countries in the peace-keeping role.

Both Greece and Turkey accepted the original proposal, but Cyprus, which is not a NATO member, rejected the idea as
Continued on Page 70, Column 5

Dutch Princess Engaged to Bourbon Prince

Queen Juliana of the Netherlands and Prince Bernhard appear at Soestdijk Palace with their daughter Princess Irene and her fiancé, Prince Carlos Hugo of Bourbon-Parma. At right is Princess Christina of the Netherlands.

4 U. S. Educators Deported by Ghana On Spying Charges

By LLOYD GARRISON
Special to The New York Times

LAGOS, Nigeria, Feb. 8—The Government of Ghana deported today four American faculty members and two other foreign teachers at the University of Ghana today for allegedly "indulging in subversive activities."

Among those ordered expelled was Prof. William Harvey, dean of Ghana's Law School, who is on leave from the University of Michigan Law School.

The expulsions were announced over the Ghana radio as more than 2,600 members of the ruling Convention People's party invaded the university campus at Legon carrying anti-American placards and chants of "Down with Yankee slang-ism," and "C.I.A. students go home."

Witnesses said the students stood by in stony silence as the crowd invaded the campus hall, and several dormitories a number of windows were reported to have been broken in Legon hall.

A Nigerian television cameraman was roughed up and his camera seized. But there was no fighting between the demonstrators and students, who marched off singing five-hour session and then dispersed.

Mr. O'Brien was formerly chief of the United Nations force in Katanga. He resigned from the post in 1961 after having charged that foreign pres-
Continued on Page 2, Column 5

100 SOMALIS SLAIN IN ETHIOPIA CLASH

200 Are Reported Wounded as Border Fight Flares — Emergency Is Declared

By Reuters

ADDIS ABABA, Ethiopia, Feb. 8—One hundred Somalis have been killed and 200 wounded in border clashes with Ethiopian armed forces, the Government said here today.

Nine Ethiopians were reported killed and 14 wounded. The fighting occurred yesterday around the town of Tug Wajale, which lay on both sides of the border.

The Government said the Somalis were putting pressure on 10 Ethiopian posts along the border and that Tug Wajale had been raided. Fighting was reported to have broken out again today.

Ethiopia declared a state of emergency on the Somali border and Emperor Haile Selassie sent an urgent message to African heads of state to impose a ban on the fighting.

The Emperor described the situation as "the latest in a series of incidents which have been provoked by armed bands
Continued on Page 5, Column 3

Irene Renounces Her Rights To Throne to Resolve Crisis

By The Associated Press

THE HAGUE, Sunday, Feb. 9—Princess Irene renounced today her rights to the Netherlands throne and decided to live in exile rather than give up marriage to the man of her heart, a Roman Catholic Spanish prince.

Her fiancé, Carlos Hugo of Bourbon-Parma, was with her when the Princess made the decision at a conference today at Soestdijk Palace.

Premier Victor G. M. Marijnen announced to the public the opinions of the crisis and the decision of the most dramatic royal romance since Britain's King Edward VIII abdicated in 1936 to marry Mrs. Wallis Simpson. The palace conference ended about 3 A.M.

The Premier and the two Prince Bernhard, and the two meeting seeking to find a solution to the romance that rocked the throne of the Netherlands.

For the first time since the disastrous floods of 1953 the Dutch radio broke its rigid ban tonight to give out the news.

Irene was next in line of succession to the throne after her sister Crown Princess Beatrix.

LATINS ARE IRKED BY U.S. RECEPTION

Delegates to Pan American Parley Say Washington's Interest in Area Ebbs

By HENRY RAYMONT
Special to The New York Times

WASHINGTON, Feb. 8—Sixty delegates to the third Pan American Interparliamentary Conference left today, most of them believing that they had marched less than comfortable warmth to the United States.

In public and private statements, Senators and Deputies from eight Latin-American countries saw in this an indication that Washington's concern for their area is waning.

Again and again the delegates complained that Latin America seemed to gain scarcely half as much proportionate basis out of its attention to the threat of Cuba and Communism or, more recently, to the content of getting support to help solve the United States-Panama crisis.

U.S. EASES STAND ON GUANTANAMO; SEES END OF PERIL

Capital Now Doubts Theory That Havana Sent Boats to Florida as a Pretext

WATER TANKERS ON WAY

Pentagon Acts to Eliminate Reliance on Cuban Supply — Base Reported Calm

By MAX FRANKEL
Special to The New York Times

WASHINGTON, Feb. 8—The Administration took a much calmer view today of the United States' dispute with Cuba and moved to end the exchange of retaliatory harassments.

Officials, let it be known that they were inclined to doubt the theory that Premier Fidel Castro had provoked them into seizing four Cuban fishing boats to justify a series of actions against the United States naval base at Guantanamo Bay.

In any case, Washington does not expect further trouble at the base.

The United States will carry on with measures to make Guantanamo independent of Cuban water and power supplies, but it has also urged authorities in Florida to deal quickly and leniently with the captured vessels and crewmen, hoping to end the affair, which more seriously than it became menacing only 24 hours ago.

Water Called a Reply

The base had 35 fishermen were seized 65 miles west of Key West, Fla., Sunday. Eventually they were turned over to state officials for prosecution under a Florida law against smuggling and fishing in territorial waters.

On Thursday, Cuba responded by cutting off Guantanamo's attractive program for the civilian workers at Guantanamo's waters, too.

Yesterday Washington complained when orders to forgo reliance on Cuban water and to cut off the flow of dollars from the base to the Cuban Government. This would jeopardize the jobs of 2,500 Cuban workers who commute to the base and who surrender their dollar wages to a Cuban bank.

Administration Moves Fast

The Administration moved fast and halted tough yesterday officials said, because it had to have the possibility of a major effort to challenge the Cuban naval installation.

Premier Castro has consistently challenged the legality of the base on Cuban soil, but has thus far vowed only legal and diplomatic measures to end the United States lease.

The requests here yesterday were that the Cuban fishing boats be intentionally aided into United States waters, with Havana's knowledge and approval. The strategy apparently seemed determined to look the affair with the Guantanamo question and to make
Continued on Page 57, Column 1

Today's Sections

[Index listing, columns of sections and page numbers]

Sports News

WINTER OLYMPICS

The Soviet Union's team won the gold medal in hockey at the Winter Olympics in Innsbruck, Austria, by beating the Canadians, 3—2, in their final game of the round-robin tournament yesterday.

Americans turned in surprise performances by finishing second and third in the men's slalom. Bruce Kidd of Vermont and Jimmy Heuga of California was third. Josef Stiegler of Austria took the gold medal.

A Swedish quartet captured the title in the 40-kilometer ski relay. The American team placed fifth.

HORSE RACING

Top Gallant and Admiral Vee finished in a dead heat for first in the $81,900 Seminole Handicap at Hialeah Park. The favored Mongo was fifth. Top Gallant paid $18 for $2 to win the and Admiral Vee returned $6.

BASKETBALL

St. John's upset Loyola of Chicago, 71—68; Yale defeated Columbia, 73—67, and New York University routed Brandeis, 88—67.

HOCKEY

The Montreal Canadiens, National League leaders, crushed the New York Rangers here, 6—2.

Savagery Marks Tribal Warfare in Rwanda

Watusi, Once Feudal Lords, Flee to Neighboring Lands — Bahutu Kill Thousands

By ROBERT CONLEY
Special to The New York Times

KIGALI, Rwanda, Feb. 8—The savagery that has swept through this mountainous African land marks the most By authoritative accounts, at least 10,000 Watusi men, women and children perished in the last massacres here.

The Watusi, who often reach seven feet in height, were Rwanda's feudal overlords for more than four centuries. Now they are fleeing the Bahutu, a tribe of shorter people who rose against their former vassals.

About 23,000 more Watusi are reported to have fled to neighboring Tanganyika, Uganda, Burundi and the Congo.

The Watusi have been beaten, clubbed and hacked to death to an extent that one investigator approached pressedle, the international eradication of a tribe.

Some are said to have been poisoned, while others were shot. Bodies appear to have been thrown by the hundreds into Rwanda's rivers, which are thick with crocodiles.

One missionary reported hav-
Regime Said to Permit Raids as Reprisals for Terrorism by Monarchist Guerrillas

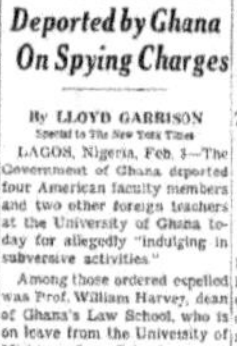

ning of a Watusi stronghold destruction.

In that attack a guerrilla band of Watusi critics, armed with rifles, bows and arrows, invaded from Burundi in the south and nearly seized the capital before being routed by the Rwanda Army.

Other tribal bands—called Inyenzi, or "cockroaches," because they strike at night—attacked the Watusi from Uganda in the north and the Congo across Lake Kivu on the west. In one such attack, a band was seized running 30 Watusi political leaders and to be chosen before battling the revolutionary government.

At least 500 Watusi guerrillas were killed in battles with the Rwanda Army, apart from those seized.

The guerrilla casualties were said to include a number of deserters from the Congolese Army.

Amid charges and counter-charges over the massacres and guerrilla raids, Rwanda and Burundi have virtually broken diplomatic relations.

Burundi not her own soil, was
Continued on Page 77, Column 3

Big Canarsie Tract Freed for Housing

By EDITH EVANS ASBURY

One of the few large tracts of vacant land in the city publicly attached the Watusi from Uganda in the north and the Congo across Lake Kivu on the west, in the Canarsie section of Brooklyn, was freed yesterday for building of medium- and low-income housing construction in small areas has been available for development as a result of years of calling last week.

But the tract is still a subject of controversy.

The tract, 161 acres in the Paerdegat Basin of the Flatlands section of Brooklyn, was over-owned by the city. Its use on July 13, 1961, the City Planning Commission apportioned as an ideal inside for housing backed by the city and state. However, in the last 10 years the city has used two-thirds of its holdings in the area, should the city decide to reappropriate the
Continued on Page 55, Column 1

New York Times - February 9, 1964

Boasting the motto of "All the News That's Fit to Print," *The New York Times* began in 1851 as the *New-York Daily Times*; it became *The New-York Times* in 1857, and the hyphen wasn't dropped until 1891! The paper began publishing a Sunday edition in 1861 in order to provide information about the Civil War. Speaking of the Civil War, during the New York City draft riots of 1863, publisher Henry Raymond held the mobs back from the New York Times building (across from City Hall) with Gatling guns, one of which he manned himself!

To skip ahead nearly a century, in 1960 the paper printed an advertisement paid for by supporters of Dr. Martin Luther King which criticized the police in Montgomery, Alabama, and contained several inaccuracies (about the number of times Dr. King had been arrested, the song some protesters were singing, etc.). This ad led to Montgomery police commissioner L.B. Sullivan suing the *Times* and winning a defamation suit (and $500,000) in the Alabama courts. The decision was appealed to the Supreme Court, and in March 1964, in a 9-0 decision, the justices overturned the judgment against the *Times*. The case reaffirmed the First Amendment and the freedom of the press, and other pending defamation cases against the *Times* were thrown out.

Our February 9th 1964 issue has no surprises about the news of the day - the lead story was about a Dutch princess getting engaged to a Bourbon prince. There are six modules associated with this edition of *The New York Times*. Complete any or all of them.

Module 89: White Episcopalians

In an effort to integrate churches, the "White Episcopalians" were encouraged to transfer their memberships to African-American parishes. Martin Luther King has been attributed as saying that 11AM on Sundays was when America was most segregated. Has this changed in our time? Are churches still often segregated by race? Why or why not?

Module 90: Bryn Mawr and Haverford Debate on Rights

As part of a conference on "The Second American Revolution," students at Bryn Mawr and Haverford colleges sponsored a debate between segregationists and integrationists. Over 1,000 students attended. Could such a debate occur on a college campus today? Why or why not?

Module 91: Hospitals Selling Cigarettes

It seems laughable now, but as a hospital administrator in Reno said, "I don't think I can deny a paying patient the right to smoke a cigarette." The role of cigarettes in our society has changed immensely since 1964, when this was an issue of debate. What factors do you think have led to the banning of smoking and selling cigarettes (in hospitals and otherwise)? Have these changes been all for the best? Why or why not?

Module 92: Beatles in New York!

There was a report that the Plaza Hotel would not have allowed the Beatles to stay there if they had known who they were, and the Plaza refused to comment on it! And there are other interesting tidbits in this article. What do you think of Ray Block's assessment of the Beatles?

Module 93: CIA Statistics

Measuring the output of the Soviet economy was never going to be easy, but the CIA always tried. The accuracy of their assessments became something of a joke after the fall of the Soviet Union - they had been predicting 6% growth per year when the Soviet economy was stagnant and production was falling. How important was this information, and how does it relate to how we estimate the size of economies today?

Module 94: China in Africa

The seven-week trip of Zhou Enlai to 10 African countries was news in 1964, as Communist China fought for diplomatic recognition with Taiwan. How has this dynamic changed since 1964? And what is Zhou Enlai's reputation in China like today?

The New York Times Magazine

February 9, 1964   SECTION 6

STRONG MAN OF VIETNAM

"The essential point for defeating the Communists is to have the rural population with us," says Maj. Gen. Nguyen Khanh. For a picture story of Vietnam's troubles, see Pages 12 and 13.

New York Times Magazine - February 9, 1964

The creation of a Sunday "magazine" was part of a top-to-bottom overhaul of *The New York Times* by owner Adolph Ochs in 1896. The idea was that a magazine format would be a more appropriate outlet for longer stories than would (or could) be printed in the newspaper. The inaugural edition of the magazine on September 6, 1896 also featured photographs, which was a first for *The New York Times*. In fact, it was the sixteen pages of photographs celebrating Queen Victoria's Diamond Jubilee in 1897 which helped to solidify the magazine's popularity and success.

As an aside, I was utterly thrilled to find a physical copy of the February 9th 1964 edition of *The New York Times Magazine* for inclusion in this time travel experience. Who keeps a newspaper magazine in storage for decades?! In addition to the thought-provoking articles covered in the modules below, I've also included an advertisement for the New York Military Academy, where in 1964 future president Donald Trump was finishing up his senior year.

There are five modules associated with the February 9th edition of *The New York Times Magazine*. Complete any or all of them.

Module 95: Vietnam

The "dirty, untidy, disagreeable" war in Vietnam is the subject of this photo collage which spans from 1946 to Nguyen Khanh's forming of a military junta. There is a similar article in about Khanh in the February 14th issue of *Life* magazine. Research what became of Khanh's role in Vietnamese politics and his eventual fate (Hint: it wasn't so bad).

Module 96: The Negro's Problem is the White's

This essay is an interesting take on American history and the state of the Civil Rights movement in 1964. The author's conclusion is that "animosity, indifference, and neglect have characterized the attitude of the white population" and any "progress to date has been made through the economic self-interest of the white community." Do you think that this was true in 1964? Do you believe it is true in our time today? Why or why not?

Module 97: Physical Fitness Mania

This is an interesting opinion piece at a number of levels, beginning with the fact that it utterly ignores the subject of women playing sports. Putting that aside, what do you think of the author's proposals for athletes and non-athletes? His advice about cigarettes, alcohol, and eating? Do you think that this article is more of a "historical artifact" or a prediction of things to come? Finally, how could you adapt this article to our time?

Module 98: Teens Who Want to Help

While the novel idea of teenaged or "junior volunteers" are the focus of this article, it also brings up seemingly age-old questions about how government programs can be used in an attempt to make a difference in the lives of children. For example, Dr. Kenneth Clark was one of the founders of HARYOU, and Neil deGrasse Tyson's father

Cyril was the first director of the organization. Research what HARYOU accomplished and the status of the program (and others like it) now. What experiences have you had with volunteering? What aspects have been the most rewarding?

Module 99: Advertisements

It's not just the writing that's sophisticated in *The New York Times Magazine*, but the ads too! Which ad is your favorite, and why? Which ads do you think worked better in 1964 than today? What do these ads say about the typical reader of *The New York Times Magazine*?

NATIONAL

ENQUIRER

THE WORLD'S LIVELIEST PAPER

★★★ SPORTS 15¢

Vol. 38, No. 24, February 9-15, 1964

'Citizen of the Year' Steals $38,000—And Then...

BURNS PAL ALIVE TO FAKE OWN DEATH

National Enquirer - February 9, 1964

Many people believe that the *National Enquirer* is a publication of recent vintage, but it actually started as a local New York paper called the *New York Evening Enquirer* in 1926. By the early 1950s it was reduced to a weekly with a circulation of 17,000.

It wasn't until Generoso Pope bought the newspaper in 1952 that circulation took off. According to Pope's son, the money to buy the newspaper was provided by the Luciano crime family in New York on the condition that the paper print daily lottery numbers and not report any news about the Mafia.

Pope also changed the name of the newspaper in 1957 to the *National Enquirer* and focussed on sensational news and celebrity gossip, as can be seen in our February 9th headline "'Citizen of the Year' Steals $38,000 - and then BURNS PAL ALIVE TO FAKE OWN DEATH." By selling the paper exclusively at newsstands and in drugstores, by 1966 Pope was able to raise the weekly circulation to one million!

Our February 9th edition of the *National Enquirer* is a good representation of what the magazine was like in the mid-1960s. Pope would change the magazine again in 1967, toning down the blood and gore, in order to sell in supermarkets. It was another brilliant marketing move to increase circulation.

There are five modules associated with this issue of the *National Enquirer*. Complete any or all of them.

Module 100: Citizen of the Year
Although the story reads like the plot of a 1930s potboiler, Robert Domer thought he had collecting his life insurance by faking his own death all figured out. What tripped him up? If you had to plan this crime for him, what would you have done differently? Why?

Module 101: He Spit Out the Bullet!
Another sensational story, this time from Gardenia, California, where they make the police tough! Do you believe that this story could be true? Why or why not?

Module 102: Inside and Straight
This module represents one of the gossip columns from the *National Enquirer*. What is your favorite piece of "news?" Why? Mine is Judy Garland yelling at Martha Raye. No clowning around during taping!

Module 103: I Had to Kill My Husband
While some people believe that we all die alone, James Heape was NOT one of those people. He continually threatened to kill his wife as he was dying of cancer. So she shot him! Do you think that her manslaughter conviction was justified? Why or why not? How do you think the crime would be treated today?

Module 104: Running Away from Home

Unhappy 16-year-old Dave Porter apparently didn't want to move to California, so he packed up his siblings and drove to Texas! Or tried to. My favorite part of this story is where he was stopped at the Arizona border and the car was searched for plants! Do you think a story like this could happen in our time? How would it be different if it did?

billboard
1964
THE HOT 100

Top Music

Popular music is always a reflection of its time, and the second week of February 1964 was no exception. Here is some background on the songs that took up the top 5 slots in the Billboard Hot 100 for the week of February 8th. People of a certain age might want to read the following in the voice of Casey Kasem.

Topping the charts is the Beatles first #1 hit in America, "I Want to Hold Your Hand.". The song was released in late January, and had already reached the top slot the week before. It remained on the Billboard charts for the next 14 weeks!

Second on the chart (where it peaked) was "You Don't Own Me" by 17-year-old Leslie Gore. She had been successful in 1963 with the song "It's My Party," but was not to reach the Top 10 again..

The Marketts take the third position on the chart with their hit "Out of Limits." Released as an instrumental surfer song, it peaked in the #3 position on the Billboard Hot 100. The song was originally called "Outer Limits" (like the television show of that name), but Rod Sterling sued and so they changed the name. Good thing it was an instrumental!

The fourth position was taken by The Rip Chords "Hey Little Cobra," which was a an anthem to the Shelby Cobra car. The song peaked at #4 on the Hot 100.

The final position was taken by Major Lance's "Um Um Um Um Um Um," which peaked at #5 on the Hot 100 chart.

As a final note, the Beatles song "She Loves You" was ranked 7th for the week, but went on to peak at #1 on March 21st 1964.

There are two modules for this media. Complete either or both of them.

Module 105: Favorite

This is completely a matter of personal choice, but which Top 5 song is your favorite? Do you have a memory tied to any of them? What is it?

Module 106: Aging well?

Which of the Top 5 songs do you believe has aged the best? Why? And which do you think is most indicative of the music scene in 1964?

Maverick

Westerns were so popular in the 1950s and 1960s that on a weekend, television stations were able to run two reruns per day of *Maverick*! Granted, it's a great show, and made James Garner a star, but still!

Maverick was created by writer and producer Roy Huggins as a show that would follow an honest gambler and card sharp through his adventures in the American West. It was televised on ABC as counter-programming to *The Ed Sullivan Show*, but only Huggins and star James Garner thought it would succeed. Within a year, they were proven to be correct! However, there was a major problem with the show - they couldn't turn them out fast enough to meet the network's timeline. This was solved in the eighth show by providing Bret Maverick (James Garner) with a brother named Bart Maverick (played by Jack Kelly). This allowed them to use two different film crews shooting episodes at the same time. Some episodes featured Bret, some featured Bart, and some had both brothers as characters. Roy Huggins later admitted that there were no differences between the brothers - both were itinerant poker players who loved money, quoted wise advice from their "Pappy," and had a $1,000 bill pinned to the inside pocket of their coat for emergencies. This allowed the scripts to be used for whichever actor was available. If there was a difference in the episodes, it was that Garner's tended to have more comedy in them because he was a better comedic actor.

When Garner left the series in the third year to pursue more lucrative movie work, a new character was added: cousin Beau Maverick! While the part was originally offered to Sean Connery (who turned it down), it was accepted by his later 007 replacement Roger Moore! Unfortunately, Moore only lasted 14 episodes, leaving over what he felt was the lack of quality in the scripts. He was replaced by yet another Maverick brother, Brent Maverick (played by Robert Colbert). Brent was unceremoniously dropped in the last season of the show (Colbert said he wasn't even informed by the studio that he was fired) and new episodes with Jack Kelly were alternated with reruns of James Garner episodes. Incidentally, writer and producer Roy Huggins went on to develop a number of successful and critically acclaimed series for ABC, including *The Fugitive*, *77 Sunset Strip*, and *The Rockford Files* (also starring James Garner). Since he had been robbed of credit for his work earlier in his career, he negotiated what was referred to as "the Huggins contract," where he would receive credit and royalties for any material which he had conceived, even if it was produced by others. For example, he later received credit for the 1993 film *U.S. Marshals* because it was based on characters he had created for *The Fugitive*. This helped to change the power dynamics in Hollywood, and more creators demanded a "Huggins contract."

The two episodes presented on February 9th are very good! They are among the first four episodes shot during the first season, with "Point Blank" being the second episode, and "Ghost Rider" being the fourth. Therefore, they feature James Garner alone as Bret Maverick.

Rather than treat the episodes differently, they share the same modules. Complete any or all of them!

Module 107: The popularity of Westerns

The most popular genre of shows in the 1950s and 1960s was the Western, with *Gunsmoke* and *Bonanza* consistently at the top of the ratings. Why do you believe that the Westerns were so popular? What does it say about American culture of that time? And why are there no shows set in the Old West in our time (and that includes Westworld!)? What does it say about our time that people no longer care about Westerns?

Module 108: Hero or Antihero?

Bret Maverick is a gambler, a self-confessed coward (although his actions tell a different story), and often ends up incarcerated. And yet he's considered a hero! Do you feel that this is appropriate? Is he more of an "Antihero?" Why or why not?

Module 109: The portrayal of women

Women are in both *Maverick* episodes, but they are portrayed differently in each. Which episode do you feel is more in touch with the sensibilities of 1957 America (when the episode was shot)? Why? How do you think the episodes would be changed if reshot today?

The Adventures of Robin Hood

Robin Hood's love of fishing is often overlooked among his legendary exploits, but after watching this episode of the British ITV series, you'll be fully up-to-date on his ability as an angler! This series consisted of 143 half-hour episodes shot between 1955 and 1959, and the origin of the series is very interesting. Hannah Weinstein was a Leftist writer with a degree in journalism from New York University. Although she had worked as a reporter for the *New York Herald Tribune* since the 1920s, by 1950, she had moved abroad, first to Paris, and then to London. She started her own production company, Sapphire Films, with financial support she received from the American Communist Party, and then bought scripts from writers who had been blacklisted in America for their Communist affiliations, including members of the "Hollywood Ten" such as Ring Lardner and Adrian Scott. Of course they wrote under pseudonyms in order to avoid creating any controversy for the series.

The February 9th episode is titled "The Secret Pool" and originally aired on March 11, 1957. Like the rest of the series, it was shot on 35mm film (in order to look more like a movie than a television show) and had "fade-outs" where commercials could be inserted for the American market. Even though it's a midday weekend rerun, it's worth watching!

This media has three modules associated with it. Complete any or all.

Module 110: Politics
The blacklisted writers were attracted to writing for the Robin Hood series because it matched their political views of taking from the rich and giving to the poor. In what ways does this orientation evidence itself in this episode? Are the rich portrayed more as evil or stupid? Why?

Module 111: The 1950s in the 1300s
While the clothes in the Robin Hood series say "1300s," the hairstyles say 1955. That's one inaccuracy in the episode, but what others do you see?

Module 112: The ethics of Robin Hood
Stealing from a rich person is still stealing. In what ways do issues of class (and caste - noble vs. commoner) play out in this episode? What lessons can be applied to our time?

Return to Oz

Keeping with the apparent *Wizard of Oz* theme of February 9th (the *Judy Garland Show* would be on ABC three hours later) *Return to Oz* premiered on this day in 1964 as a part of *The General Electric Fantasy Hour* for children. It is the first animated special produced by Arthur Rankin Jr. and Jules Bass, who would go on to much greater popular acclaim for their stop-motion "Animagic" productions of holiday favorites like *Rudolph the Red-Nosed Reindeer*, *Frosty the Snowman* (featuring Jimmy Durante!), and *Santa Claus is Coming to Town*.

The plot involves Dorothy hearing from Glenda the Good Witch that the Wicked Witch of the West had come back to life and captured the Wizard! Dorothy would need to return to Oz, reunite with her friends, have some adventures, and defeat the Wicked Witch a second time. I will avoid any spoilers about how things turn out.

Module 113: Animation vs. "Animagic"

While *Return to Oz* is a good example of early 1960's animation - 40 animators in Toronto drew 140,000 images to create it - how do you think it stacks up against Rankin and Bass's later "Animagic" holiday specials? Why do you think the "Animagic" specials are so beloved? Which is your favorite? Why?

Module 114: Classic or crap?

While this production was presented as a continuation of the 1961 animated series *Tales of the Wizard of Oz*, and is based on the original characters author Frank Baum created, do you believe that it is a "classic?" Why or why not?

The Adventures of Ozzie and Harriet

While it began as a radio show in 1944, the television series of *The Adventures of Ozzie and Harriet* debuted on October 10th 1952 on ABC. Since the radio show had been a hit, Ozzie Nelson was able to negotiate a guaranteed 10-year contract with ABC for the television series, so that the Nelsons would continue to get paid whether the series was cancelled or not! This allowed the show to be the first primetime scripted series to reach that milestone.

Many of the storylines of the show were taken from the Nelson's own lives, and when their sons, David and Ricky, got married, their wives were incorporated into the show too! Which leads us to tonight's episode - "A Wife in the Office." The plot isn't very complex, but the backstory is. David was married to June Blair, who was the January 1957 Playboy Playmate of the Month. His brother Ricky was the best man at their 1961 wedding! They eventually divorced in 1975 after having two children.

There are two modules associated with this episode. Complete either or both of them.

Module 115: The 1950s

While the show ran for 14 seasons, with the 1963-64 being the most popular (29th in the Neilson ratings) it was cancelled in 1966 because audiences seemed to think that it represented more "50s" values than "60s" values. As you watch the show, do you believe that this is true? Why or why not?

Module 116: The Nelson's Reality Show

The Nelsons played versions of themselves, and the opening credits said that the Nelsons were "played by" the family. What do you think of the idea of incorporating new people into the show as they married into the family (even when they are the Playmate of the Month)? How is this the same and different from the reality shows of our time?

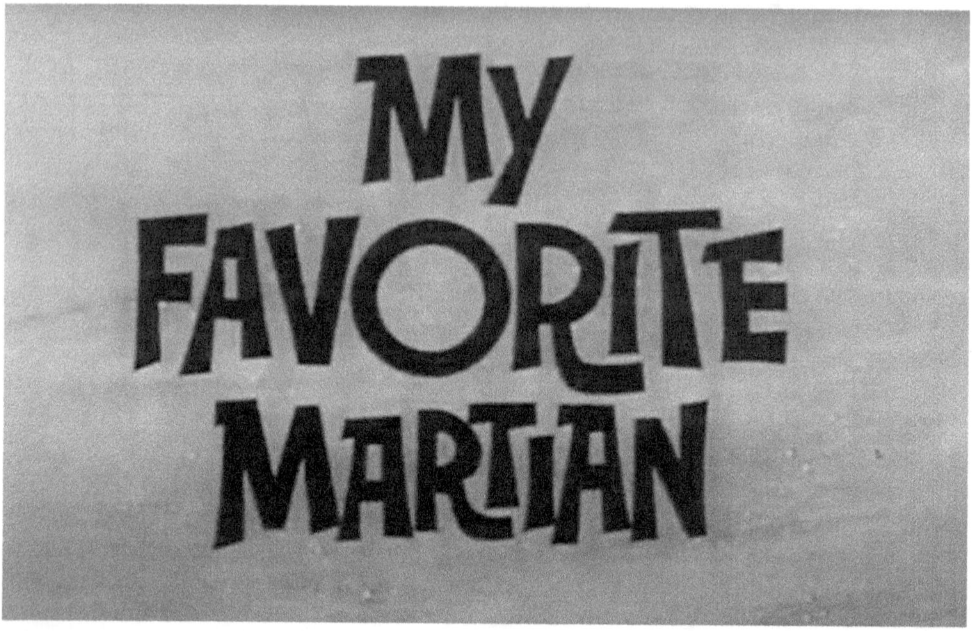
MY
FAVORITE
MARTIAN

My Favorite Martian

Although it only lasted three seasons on CBS, *My Favorite Martian* managed to influence the way that television portrayed characters. For example, as a Martian, "Uncle Martin" has a number of special powers, such as the ability to read minds, levitate objects, and become invisible. Thankfully, all of these powers are present in the February 9th episode! These unexplained "powers" can be seen in the plots of both *Bewitched* (which premiered in 1964) and *I Dream of Jeannie* (which premiered in 1965).

Our episode for tonight is from the first season, and so is in black and white. The series wasn't shot in color until the final season. Titled "Who am I?," it explores Uncle Martin getting hit on the head with a tool he has levitated, which leads to amnesia of a sort. The reason I say "of a sort" is because it doesn't match the two types of amnesia which psychologists study - retrograde amnesia (where the past is forgotten) and anterograde amnesia (where new information cannot be accessed). Anterograde amnesia is much more common, and is in many ways a natural part of aging. If you live long enough, you'll be able to recall information from 50 years ago, but won't be able to remember what happened last week. That's anterograde amnesia. However, what happens to Uncle Martin is more akin to a dissociative fugue state, which is where people lose awareness of who they are, and oftentimes wander off. But this discussion might be taking a sitcom plot from the 1960s too seriously.

There are three modules associated with this episode of *My Favorite Martian*. Complete any or all of them.

Module 117: Mr. Hand

The "Martian" star of *My Favorite Martian* was Ray Walston, a prolific stage actor who had a long career in movies and television. For most people of my generation, he's Mr. Hand, the history teacher from *Fast Times at Ridgemont High*. Similarly, his co-star, Bill Bixby, is forever the *Incredible Hulk*! How does seeing these actors in other roles impact your appreciation of *My Favorite Martian*?

Module 118: Space Aliens

My Favorite Martian is one of the first shows to feature an extraterrestrial as a main character - Mr. Spock of *Star Trek* fame wouldn't make his debut until 1966. In what ways does *My Favorite Martian* use Uncle Martin as a reflection of human motivation and behavior? How do his actions contrast with ours?

Module 119: This show today?

Could a show like *My Favorite Martian* be a hit today? Why or why not?

The Scarecrow of Romney Marsh - Part 1

While *The Scarecrow of Romney Marsh* was specifically produced for the *Walt Disney's Wonderful World of Color* show, it was also recut for a theatrical run in Great Britain during the Christmas season of 1963 under the title of *Dr. Syn, Alias the Scarecrow*. It was released as a double feature with Walt Disney's *The Sword in the Stone*. Interestingly, it was recut again for American audiences in the 1970s and released on a double bill with *Treasure Island*! So it's had a few different permutations.

Tonight is just Part 1 of the story, so if you want to see the complete movie you'll have to find it on YouTube or DVD!

There are two modules associated with this media. Complete either or both of them.

Module 120: The Song

Having watched the show, you might have noticed that one of the best things about *The Scarecrow of Romney Marsh* is the theme song! What do you think of it and why is it so catchy?

Module 121: Counterprogramming

Although 73 million people watched the Beatles on *The Ed Sullivan Show*, SOME people were watching *The Scarecrow of Romney Marsh*. But who? Who do you think the target demographic for this movie was? And was it wise to break it up into two parts, so that people would have to watch on February 9th to understand the rest of the movie on February 16th? Why or why not?

The Ed Sullivan Show

From the show's debut on June 20, 1948 with guests Dean Martin and Jerry Lewis,   was a Sunday night juggernaut associated with top-tier entertainment. This helps to explain why the Beatles chose to make their American premier on the show. However, the road to the February 9th appearance actually began in November 1963, when Ed Sullivan was in Heathrow Airport in London coincidentally when the Beatles were returning from Stockholm. Beatlemania was in full swing, and Sullivan was reminded of the craze that surrounded Elvis Presley, so he contacted Brian Epstein (the Beatles manager) and offered the Beatles a single appearance for a large fee. Epstein countered with multiple appearances for a small fee, and this is why the Beatles appeared for three consecutive Sundays starting on February 9th 1964.

The night was more than just the Beatles, and so there are eight modules associated with this episode. Complete any or all of them.

Module 122: The Beatles

The Beatles got the opening and closing slots (in addition to top billing) for the February 9th show. It was a good decision though - their appearance attracted 73 million viewers, a record at the time. And they put on a great show. Which song is your favorite? Why? And how do you feel about the "Beatlemania" era Beatles compared to their later iterations?

Module 123: Magician Fred Kaps

Can you imagine what it would be like to go on immediately after the Beatles? Yet that is what Dutch magician Fred Caps did! This was his only appearance on *The Ed Sullivan Show*, but he made it count. Which of his illusions is your favorite? Why?

Module 124: Oliver!

The Ed Sullivan Show was in many ways a vaudeville production, with a number of different acts to appeal to the widest audience possible. And what better than an adaptation of Charles Dickens *Oliver Twist* featuring future Monkees star Davy Jones as the Artful Dodger?! While it premiered in London in 1960, the Broadway production didn't reach audiences until 1963, so Ed Sullivan was timely in booking this act. What are your thoughts about the singing and staging of Oliver? And why do you think variety shows are no longer on broadcast television?

Module 125: Frank Gorshin

When I first saw Frank Gorshin on the show, I thought "Hey! That's the Riddler!" While Fred Gorshin became famous as a nightclub impressionist, he was also a frequent guest on *The Ed Sullivan Show*. Although his impressions are dated, which is your favorite? And which do you believe translate into our time? Why?

Module 126: Tessie O'Shea

With her exuberant manner and banjolele, Tessie O'Shea was a consummate entertainer. She earned her spot on *The Ed Sullivan Show* due to her casting in the 1963 Broadway musical *The Girl Who Came to Supper*. What is your favorite part of her act? Who do you see as the best example of a performer like her from our time?

Module 127: Charlie Brill and Mitzi McCall

The comedy duo of husband and wife Charlie Brill and Mitzi McCall had never heard of the Beatles when they arrived at the Ed Sullivan Theater, and thought the crowds of teenagers were there to see impressionist Fred Gorshin! At the rehearsal before the show, they did their act for Ed Sullivan in his office, and he thought that their act was too "high-brow," giving specific instructions on which bits to keep and which to drop. Distraught at having to change their act at the last possible moment, they went back to their dressing room, which was the worst in the theater, and contained a Coke vending machine. As they were rehearsing their revised act, John Lennon came in because he wanted a Coke. He didn't have a dime, so they bought him one. He sat and talked with them, sketching them as they visited. Then manager Brian Epstein came to retrieve John, and he left the portrait drawing behind for them. Brill says, "I thought 'What a pretentious guy' and threw it away."

Their act utterly bombed that night, their big shot at the big time. As you watch their revised act, do you think it's funny? Was appearing the same night as the Beatles a blessing or a curse? Why?

Module 128: Billy Wells and the Four Fays

This Australian acrobatic troupe has the distinction of containing the mom and cousins of Toni Basel, singer of the #1 1982 song "Mickey." Beyond that, one doesn't get to see acrobatic exhibitions on national television anymore. What do you think of their performance? And is there a place for this sort of entertainment on television today? Why or why not?

Module 129: Advertisements

I've included a sample of the advertisements from the February 9th episode. Which is your favorite? Are there any which you think could be broadcast today (albeit in color)? Why or why not?

The Judy Garland Show

It's difficult to imagine a movie star of Judy Garland's stature doing a television variety show for the 1963-1964 season, and even more difficult to believe that it was cancelled by the network. The reason? *Bonanza*. But more on that later!

I don't believe that I need to provide a mini-biography for Judy Garland, but suffice it to say that she was a major star of the 1930s and 1940s for her roles in the *Andy Hardy* movies with Mickey Rooney and perhaps most famously, her role as Dorothy in *The Wizard of Oz*. But her studio, Metro-Goldwyn-Meyer, never really knew what to do with her "girl-next-door" looks, and studio chief Louis B. Meyer referred to her as "my little hunchback." She had problems showing up late (or not at all) for films, and was released from her MGM contract in 1950, after 15 years with the studio.

She made a comeback doing theater work in the early 1950s, and made *A Star is Born* in 1954. She began doing television concerts and performed in Las Vegas for $55k per week (the record at that time). She was approached by CBS in 1961 to do a series of concert specials which were a big hit. That led to the proposal for a series - a $24 million offer for four years!

The series was troubled, and ran through three producers and one co-star (Jerry Van Dyke) in the one year it was broadcast. While it began as a variety show which featured skits, comedy, and music, by the midpoint of the 26 episode run it was just Judy Garland in concert every week. Both audiences and critics preferred the concerts, with *The New York Times* opining that "after five months of trial and error in which the show has been subjected to various and ill-fated formulas, CBS is going to let Miss Garland do what she does best - sing."

The February 9th episode, thankfully, is a "concert episode" of *The Judy Garland Show*, and was filmed in Hollywood at the CBS Television City Studios on January 24, 1964. A few days prior to the taping, Judy Garland had announced the cancellation of the series so that she could "give my children the time and attention they need." However, the reality was that her show was being crushed in the ratings every week by *Bonanza*, the #1 show on television. She had hoped that the television series would bail her out financially (she had major tax liabilities going back to the early 1950s), but this was not to be.

There are four modules associated with this show. Complete any or all of them!

Module 130: On screen costume changes

Several times during the show Judy goes behind a panel for a costume change (including makeup!) and talks with the audience about the show and being a performer, as well as the fact that most people are watching *Bonanza*. Do you feel that these interludes are more for her or for us? Are her frustrations with her costumes about the costumes, or about the cancellation of her show?

Module 131: Nostalgia vs. corney

Judy announces that "some of the songs you're going to hear tonight are somewhat nostalgic, and to some people that means corney, but as far as I'm concerned, being nostalgic is . . . a nifty way of life." As you watch her perform these classic songs, do you find them to be more "nostalgic" or "corney?" Why?

Module 132: Singing to her children

Among the hats Judy Garland was expected to wear were "entertainer" as well as "devoted mother." She even announced in the cancellation of her show that she wanted to spend more time with her children. How does singing her sing to them make you feel? Is it sincere or staged? Why?

Module 133: Favorite song

There are a number of wonderful songs in this concert. Which is your favorite? Why? What is it about Judy's delivery that makes it special?

Bonanza

Audiences loved spending time with the Cartwright family throughout the 1960s, with *Bonanza* ranking in the top three shows every year for the entire decade, and #1 from 1964-1967. The show was the first series to be shot and broadcast in color, and ran for 431 episodes from 1959 until 1973. It continues to play today in reruns.

To give a little background (although none is needed to follow tonight's episode), *Bonanza* is about the life of widower Ben Cartwright (played by Lorne Greene) and his three sons (all from different mothers) and their adventures on the enormous Ponderosa Ranch on Lake Tahoe in Nevada in the 1860s. The sons are played by three talented actors. The eldest, Adam, was played by Parnell Roberts until he left the series during the 1966 season. Why would he want to leave a hit series? The workload! While most series put out 22 episodes per season, Bonanza turned out 34! Roberts also didn't like the way his character, a man in his 30s(!), was always seeking the approval of his father - he felt the character should be more independent. The middle son is the loveable Hoss, who was played by Dan Blocker until he passed away after an operation in 1972. The youngest son, Little Joe, is played by Michael Landon, who also wrote and directed a number of episodes of *Bonanza* before moving on to *Little House on the Prairie* in 1974.

The February 9th 1964 episode ("The Cheating Game") is a good one, and unique in several ways. First, Michael Landon doesn't appear in the episode at all! Dan Blocker doesn't either, but it was more unusual for Little Joe to miss an episode - he only missed 14 episodes in the whole 431 series run.

The other amazing thing about this episode involves the character of ranch owner Laura Dayton, played by Kathie Browne. It was unusual for any of the Cartwrights to have a "love interest," and unfortunately for the women, they usually died, were killed, or ran off with someone else. However, Parnell Roberts was thinking of leaving the show in 1964, and so Laura Dayton became a recurring character, appearing in four episodes. The idea was that Adam would marry Laura and move off somewhere else. In that way, Parnell Roberts could leave the series, but still come back every once in a while for a guest appearance. An additional Cartwright character, Ben's nephew Will Cartright, was introduced in the 1964 season as a replacement for Roberts leaving the show. Will was played by Guy Williams, who went on to play the father on *Lost in Space*! When Parnell Roberts decided that he wanted to stay on *Bonanza*, there were too many Cartwrights, and Laura Dayton fell in love with Will Cartwright! Then they ran off together and were never seen again. When Roberts left the series the next year, his character was said to have gone "off to sea."

A final amazing thing about this episode is that actress Kathie Browne had appeared on *Bonanza* TWICE before! In the 1962 season she had played Hoss's love interest, banker's daughter Margie Owens. Hoss wants to marry her, but she wants to see the world, and so runs off with a travelling stranger, who takes her to San Francisco and leaves her broke and pregnant. However, we are supposed to feel bad for Hoss!

This episode includes three modules. Complete any or all of them.

Module 134: Is Adam "running the ranch?"

The portrayal of the relationship between Adam Cartwright and Laura Dayton fits television in 1964, but does it correspond to dating relationships in rural Nevada in the 1860s? Is he leading her on throughout this episode? Why DOESN'T he want to marry her? How many beautiful, available women live that close to the Ponderosa?! Do you believe that the story deals with a romantic relationship in a realistic way? Why or why not?

Module 135: The elaborate scheme

Ward Bannister shows up at Laura Dayton's ranch as a friend of her dead husband with a $10,000 life insurance policy in his pocket. But does he really know her husband? Why would HE have the insurance policy? How has Laura Dayton never heard of this trusted friend?!

It turns out to be all part of a confidence scheme to part her from the $10,000 insurance payout, which may or may not actually exist. Get her to invest in the San Francisco-Monterey Railroad! But don't cash her check for $8,000! Then murder your partner.

This plot makes no sense to me, but I may be expecting too much from a *Bonanza* script. What do you see as the plot holes in this episode? How could they have been better resolved?

Module 136: Father knows best

A troubled Adam stares into the fire and is asked by his father, "Can I help?" After explaining his misgivings about the railroad deal, Ben asks "Is it important for you to be welcome at the Running D [Ranch]?" Given the fact that Ben is a widower with three unmarried sons, why would he be discouraging them visiting with beautiful local women to play cribbage? Why does he want his grown children to remain single? What do you believe his motivations to be?

What's My Line?

If you love celebrity panel shows, then *What's My Line?* is for you! While it originally ran as a primetime show on CBS from 1950 to 1967, it enjoyed an afterlife as a daily syndicated show until 1975. It has had a number of subsequent revivals!

Today's show is interesting because of the celebrities. First, the panel. Bobby Darren was famous for his songs, such as "Splish Splash," "Mack the Knife," and "Beyond the Sea," but also for his marriage to Sandra Dee. Dorothy Kilgallen was a journalist (mostly business and gossip) and was a part of *What's My Line?* from the first show in 1950. Bennett Cerf ("or *What's My Line's* answer to the Beatles") was a the co-founder of Random House Publishing, and appeared on *What's My Line?* weekly for 17 years. As can be seen in this episode, he was well known for his awful puns (e.g. "Absinth makes the heart grow Fonda")! Finally, it wouldn't be *What's My Line?* without Arlene Francis, who was a panelist on from the second show in 1950 through the end of syndication in 1975.

The Mystery Guest, Jane Fonda, started her career on Broadway and soon moved on to Hollywood. In 1964 she was promoting her film *Sunday in New York*, so the panelists were quickly able to identify the daughter of Henry Fonda.

The fact that this episode was filmed and broadcast live on February 9th makes it an interesting time capsule of the impact the Beatles were having on pop culture in 1964.

This episode has three modules. Complete any or all of them.

Module 137: Favorite celebrity

Panel shows are great because they can reveal who is able to "think on their feet" and who is inevitably lost. This is even more clear when the panel is made up of celebrities. Who is your favorite celebrity on this episode? Why?

Module 138: The cues and clues

Besides the ages of the celebrities, what are the clues that this game show was filmed six decades ago? Is it the way they are dressed? The hairstyles? The topics they discuss? Which, if any, or the people look and act like they could be from our own time?

Module 139: The Beatles

Several times during the show, people make references to the Beatles. While none of their jokes are particularly funny, they're trying to stay hip and current. Who would you reference if you wanted to do the same in our time? Why?

The Beatles Partying in NYC

After shooting their appearance on *The Ed Sullivan Show*, the Beatles went out for a night on the town at The Peppermint Lounge. Opened in 1958 in Manhattan, the Peppermint Lounge was credited with starting the "peppermint twist" dance craze, with Sam Cooke's 1962 song "Twistin' the Night Away" referring indirectly to the club.

Ringo, however, is dancing to Barrett Strong's 1959 "Money (That's What I Want)." The Beatles had recorded a cover of the song in 1963!

There are two modules associated with this media. Complete either or both of them.

Module 140: Ringo's Dancing Ability

There isn't much opportunity to dance when you're a drummer, so it's fun to see Ringo cutting loose on the dance floor. How would you critique his dancing at The Peppermint Lounge?

Module 141: The Girl

One girl in particular goes from dancing with her friends to sitting on Ringo's lap (and maybe getting smuggled into their hotel suite). What do you think of her? What must it have been like to go from a night at a club to partying with the hottest musical group on the planet?

Debriefing

The third section is dedicated to reflecting on February 9th 1964. What have we learned about the day? What did the people of that time think was important? And how was that time similar and different from our own?

The Debriefing begins with print media which came out on February 10th (*Newsweek* and *Sports Illustrated*) as well as the Universal International Newsreel from that day. These provide us with more information about the previous week.

The complete Beatles concert in Washington, D.C. is included, as it occurred on February 11th..

The print media continues with *Time* and *Life* (from February 14th) and *The Saturday Evening Post* (from February 15th), followed by videos of celebrities reflecting on their encounters with the Beatles.

The Debriefing continues with a section on Reading What the Beatles Read, and concludes with questions about the time travel experience itself - favorites, reflections, and what has been learned.

Newsweek

FEBRUARY 10, 1964   30c

DE GAULLE'S FRANCE:
A Return To Greatness?

Newsweek - February 10, 1964

Charles de Gaulle graces the cover of the February 10th issue of *Newsweek*, and he is also the subject of one of the seven modules for this issue of the magazine. Since the history of *Newsweek* was covered for the February 3rd issue, this section will just cover the modules for the February 10th edition.

Module 142: War in Vietnam

This article goes into some detail about the status of the war in Vietnam and the tactics used to fight the Viet Cong. What decisions by LBJ in 1964 assured the fall of Saigon in 1975? Or didn't it matter what the American government did in this conflict? Why?

Module 143: School integration

The Cleveland schools were bussing 800 Black students to predominantly white schools, and then keeping them in segregated classrooms. Issues with school integration in New York, Atlanta, and Chapel Hill weren't much better. How are the racial issues of 1964 similar and different to the racial issues of today? Have things gotten better, worse, or pretty much stayed the same? Why?

Module 144: The Beckwith trial

Medgar Evers, who was the head of the Mississippi state NAACP, was murdered on June 12, 1963 by Byron de La Beckwith, a fertilizer salesman and member of the White Citizens' Council of Jackson, Mississippi. This article is shocking enough, but only refers to the first trial of "Delay" Beckwith. Research the trials and how long it took to bring Beckwith to justice.

Module 145: France's return to "greatness"

The recognition of "Red" China by France was big news in early 1964, but Charles de Gaulle went far beyond that, declaring that Europe was "in a position to offer developing countries an alternative to the rival ideologies of the U. S. and Russia." Change out "China" for "Russia" and how different is this from our situation today? Do you believe that a "revitalized Europe" is in any more of a position to provide leadership to the world today than it was in 1964? Why or why not?

Module 146: Year of the transplant

Kidney transplants were on the "surgical frontier" of medicine in 1964, but not as much as the chimpanzee heart transplant which occurred on January 24, 1964. Yet the article is skeptical about whether "animal grafts" will ever be made feasible. Research the way surgeon James Hardy was treated by colleagues after his chimpanzee heart transplant surgery (it's a fascinating story) and also look into some of the breakthroughs of transplant surgery in our own time.

Module 147: Don't fence him in!

   The level of sexism in this article is pretty amazing, but this is a great article for illustrating what academic researchers of the time thought about the social trends they saw playing out in their time. Who's predictions turned out to be more correct? Why?

Module 148: Advertisements

   The automobiles of 1964 are beautiful and amazing - just look at their advertising! You don't have to be a "car person" to know what you like, so of the advertised cars, which would you choose and why?

FEBRUARY 10, 1964   25 CENTS

Sports Illustrated

OLYMPIC SKI CHAMPION
EGON ZIMMERMANN

Sports Illustrated - February 10, 1964

For anyone who loves sports, *Sports Illustrated* (or *SI*) has been a weekly source of sports news since 1954. The addition of the "swimsuit issue" later in 1964 made *SI* part of the cultural conversation. However, the history of the magazine is more complicated.

The magazine was originally started in 1936 with a focus on "sportsmen," meaning a focus on golf, tennis, and boat racing (or all things!). The logistics of printing at the time meant that *SI* was a monthly, as the public had newspapers for daily sports news. When the original publisher sold *SI* in 1949, it only lasted another six issues.

It was Henry Luce, the publisher of *Time*, who saw the potential of the magazine. While many people advised him that there wasn't enough sports news to justify a weekly magazine, he felt that the time was right, and relaunched *Sports Illustrated* in 1954. Luce wasn't even a sports fan, and his critics were correct - *SI* lost money for over a decade. But the advent of televised sports created a market for the magazine. Right place, right time.

The cover of the February 10th issue features Olympic ski champion Egon Zimmerman of Austria. Renowned for his good looks, he won the downhill competition by 0.74 seconds! He passed away in 2019.

There are six modules for this edition of *Sports Illustrated*. Complete any or all of them.

Module 149: Scorecard

The Scorecard section provides news tidbits from the world of sports. Which is your favorite piece of news? Mine is the network contracts to broadcast NFL football - $28.2 million (or $240 million inflation-adjusted) for CBS to broadcast NFL games and $36 million (or $305 million inflation-adjusted) for NBC to broadcast AFL games. As of 2019, each TEAM receives $255 million in compensation from the league for television rights.

Module 150: Winter Olympics

The IX Winter Olympics in Innsbruck, Austria were in the news in February 1964. Although any and all records set there have probably been shattered for decades, I thought I would include it to illustrate how writing about the Olympics has changed. For example, this article is primarily about French and Russian athletes. Do you think an article like this would be written today for an American audience/ Why or why not?

Module 151: Regal Splendor on the Sidelines

It's unimaginable in our time that a royal would appear in public in a coat and hat made from an actual animal, especially a leopard. How do you feel about this display and people who continue to wear fur today? What do you think changed from 1964 to today to make wearing fur so unacceptable?

Module 152: Golf

Jack Nicklaus, Arnold Palmer, and Chi Chi Rodriguez were all in their prime in 1964 - so why weren't they winning?! At least Palmer could blame it on quitting smoking. If you're a golf fan, you're likely to find this article to be wonderful, and if you're not you won't know any of the people mentioned in it. Regardless, compare and contrast the coverage of golf from 1964 to today. When was the game better? Why?

Module 153: Sonny Liston

Sonny Liston fought Muhammad Ali (at the time known as Cassius Clay) as a 7-1 favorite on February 25, 1964. Spoiler alert! - He lost. In their rematch on May 25, 1965, Liston was knocked out in the first round. How accurate was the analysis by the men who had fought him? How does it compare to the analysis of Sonny Liston in *Police Gazette*?

Module 154: Car advertising

Sports Illustrated's advertisers knew their target market when it came to cars. In this sample of ads, which is your favorite? Which car would you pick to have today? The Porsche cost $4,200 (or $36,00 inflation-adjusted) and you would have a difficult time picking a 1964 Porsche up today for less than $120,000!

Universal International News - February 10, 1964

The Universal International News newsreels were discussed earlier in this book, and so only the three modules will be presented here. Complete any or all of them.

Module 155: Cyprus Crisis
I think that it would be difficult for most people to find Cyprus on a map (I know I couldn't), but it was in the news in February 1964. It's interesting the way "terrorist" and "extremist" were as much a part of the vocabulary in 1964 as they are in our time. For this module, research how the Cyprus Crisis was resolved.

Module 156: The Beatles Arrive!
Beatlemania is a big enough story to make it to the newsreel! The teen excitement over the Beatles was almost always compared to that of Frank Sinatra and Elvis Pressley. Do you feel that this is fair or accurate? And was all the attention easier for the Beatles because there were four of them? Why or why not?

Module 157:Scott Allen Wins the Bronze
A fourteen-year-old American figure skater was beaten for the Silver medal by a French skater who fell down three (3!) times! It made the crowd "boo!" An Olympic crowd! Research what happened to Scott Allen - his story is an interesting one.

The Beatles Concert in Washington, D.C. - February 11, 1964

After their success in New York, the Beatles boarded a train for Washington D.C. for a sold out concert at the Washington Coliseum. The train trip was necessary because a snowstorm had closed down most flights; however, 2,000 fans braved the eight inches of snow to greet them at Union Station.

As to the concert itself, it was performed "in-the-round," so that the Beatles moved around - at different times they were facing different groups of fans. This created some problems with Ringo's drum riser, as it had to be physically turned every few songs. Another issue was that Washington newspapers had reported that the Beatles loved jelly beans, and so fans pelted them with jelly beans throughout the show! According to George Harrison, "every now and again, one would hit a string on my guitar and plonk off a bad note as I was trying to play."

There are two modules associated with this media. Complete either or both of them.

Module 158: The Set List

It is interesting that the Beatles chose to play some covers along with their own material. Which is your favorite? Why? What other cover songs do you wish they had played?

Module 159: The Fans

As this was the start of Beatlemania in America, they were able to play in front of a relatively small audience in Washington, D.C. (about 8,000 fans). As their popularity increased, they began playing stadiums, and then stopped because with all of the screaming, they couldn't hear themselves play. What do you think would have been the ideal venue for the Beatles to play if they came to your town? Why? And how much would you pay to see them live?

136

Time - February 14, 1964

Marina Oswald, the Russian-born bride of presidential assassin Lee Harvey Oswald, graces the cover of this week's *Time* magazine, and is also the subject of one of the modules. Since the history of *Time* magazine was covered in the February 7th edition, this section will just cover the modules for the February 14th edition.

Module 160: The 1964 Civil Rights bill

The Civil Rights Act of 1964 was a monumental piece of legislation that is summarized in this brief article about actions to stop it in the House of Representatives. Other than racism, why might a House member be opposed to the law? The bill overcame a Senate filibuster (passing 73-27) and was signed into law by President Johnson on July 2nd.

Module 161: The Oswalds

This is a great long-form article on Marina and Marguerite Oswald's perspectives on the Warren Commission and the investigation into the assassination of JFK - "Everyone has sympathy for Mrs. Kennedy. Doesn't anyone feel sorry for me?" After reading this article, do you feel more sympathy for Marina and Marguerite Oswald? Or less? Why?

Module 162: The murder of Medgar Evers

Medgar Evers was murdered on June 12, 1963, but the man who killed him went free in February 1964 on account of a hung jury (which voted 7-5 for acquittal). Research more about what happened to Byron de la Beckwith and where he died. Was justice served in this case?

Module 163: Top pop mop-tops

The fact that *Time's* Beatles news is a week old gives some insight into the editorial turn-around time at a major magazine in 1964. What do you think of the way the Beatles are portrayed in this article?

Module 164: The behavioral sciences and the Beatles

If you want a "plain-English compendium of behavioral science's best tested propositions," look no further! Do you believe that these findings are still valid in our time? Why or why not? And which of the findings stands out the most to you? Why?

LIFE

WINTER OLYMPICS
A SOARING SKI JUMP
AT INNSBRUCK

FEBRUARY 14 · 1964 · 25¢

Life - February 14, 1964

Since I have already written about the history of *Life* magazine for the February 7th issue, I will just write about the cover of the February 14th issue, and then get to the modules. The cover features an unknown skier launching off of the Bergisel jump in Innsbruck, Austria.

While the interior contains pictures of the now forgotten Winter Olympics competitors, I thought that the other articles were more interesting, and will just provide the medal count here. Basically, the Americans did not have an impressive showing at Innsbruck! A total of seven (7!) medals and only one gold, which went to skier Terry McDermott in the Men's 500 metres. The big winner of the Winter Olympics was the Soviet Union, with a total of 25 medals, including 11 gold.

There are only two modules associated with the February 14th issue of Life magazine. Complete either or both of them.

Module 165: A Tough Little General

Like the article in *The New York Times Magazine*, the focus is on "tough little general" Nguyen Khanh. How do you think the coverage of the Vietnam conflict differs between the two magazines? Which is more "realistic?" And what do you think about the coverage of the Viet Cong?

Module 166: The Emptiness of Too Much Leisure

There seems to have been a thought in 1964 that we were entering an era when everyone in America would soon be able to just kick back and not work so hard anymore - 600 billion more hours of leisure by the year 2000! Do you feel that we are now in the Age of Leisure predicted by the author? Why or why not? Also, what do you believe the article gets right and wrong about the nature of leisure time, both in 1964 and today?

POST

THE SATURDAY EVENING POST FEBRUARY 15 · 1964 20c

Exclusive:
THE PHILBY SPY CASE
New details in the scandal that shocked Britain
when a top agent betrayed the West

A modern sea story by
NICHOLAS MONSARRAT
Author of THE CRUEL SEA

An intimate look at SOPHIA LOREN
Her views on life, love and marriage

Untold story of L.B.J.'s first weeks / Coin craze / A famous writer says hunting is humane

The Saturday Evening Post - February 14, 1964

Although it was first published in Philadelphia in 1821, *The Saturday Evening Post* was past its prime by 1964, with weekly sales dropping considerably since the late 1950s. Why? Blame television and politics. The long-form journalism featured in *The Saturday Evening Post* had a difficult time competing for eyeballs with *Bonanza*, and the editorial staff's conservative bent was out of step with the times. By 1968 the magazine was losing $5 million per year, and ceased publication in 1969. Although it has gone through several revivals, the magazine is far from the glory days of Norman Rockwell covers, and is currently published six times per year.

There are only three modules associated with the February 15th issue of *The Saturday Evening Post*. Complete any or all of them.

Module 167: Hunting

In 1964, hunting was "under attack" by the "various kinds of puritans with whom the culture of this country is traditionally afflicted." So believes the article's author, American novelist and playwright Vance Bourjaily. What do you think of his arguments? Are they different from the arguments which would be made today? As a coda, Bourjaily's son Phil grew up to write a column for Field & Stream!

Module 168: Sophia Loren

Sophia Loren was one of the most famous actresses in 1964, and is also in a feature article in this month's *Screen Stories* magazine. While the article is sure to provide her measurements (38-24-38), it also provides an interesting biography of how she became a film actress and star. What do you think was the most interesting part of the article? And which actress from our time is closest to Sophia Loren in looks and ability? Why?

Module 169: Advertisements

From cars to Coke, the advertisements in *The Saturday Evening Post* reflect the products Americans aspired to own in 1964. Which of the ads do you believe is the most effective? Why? Do you think any of the ads could be run in our time for similar products? Why or why not?

Celebrity Reminiscences About the Beatles

While many, many people have reminiscences about the impact that the Beatles had on them, I thought I would include just a few to close out this section.

Module 170: Whoopi Goldberg

Whoopi Goldberg has some interesting insights about the place of the Beatles in her life. Examine your own thoughts about the impact the Beatles have had on you. How has becoming familiar with them and their music changed you?

Module 171: Sigourney Weaver

Sigourney Weaver gives a good description of what it was like to be caught up in Beatlemania as a teenager. Do you think you would have reacted similarly? Have you ever felt the same about a celebrity or musician? Who was it and how did they impact you?

Module 172: Mitzi Gaynor

Mitzi Gaynor got top billing over the Beatles for *The Ed Sullivan Show* that was broadcast on February 16th 1964, and discusses the experience in this video. I like the story about her husband yelling at Paul to "get that girl off the stage!" Which of her stories is your favorite? Why?

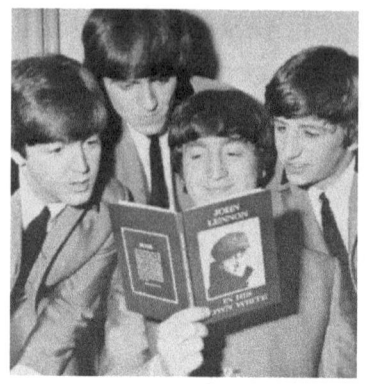

Reading What the Beatles Read

While it is part of the time travel experience of February 9th 1964, it's also fun to consider what the Beatles *themselves* were reading in 1964, which will be the subject of these modules. How do we know what media they were consuming? Photographs of them WITH the media. Each of the following modules is accompanied by a photo, so you can read what the Beatles read, contemporaneous with 1964!

In His Own Write by John Lennon - The Writing Beatle!
John Lennon had aspirations as an artist beyond just music, as can be seen in this mostly unreadable book. With an introduction by Paul, and "illustrations" by artist Robert Freeman, *In His Own Write* is a non-linear series of sketches which don't make a whole lot of sense individually or collectively, but are a reflection of John's writing interests.

Module 173: The stories
Which do you believe is the most interesting story? Why? Do you believe that this book was a serious writing endeavor, or just an opportunity to cash in on the popularity of the Beatles? Why or why not?

Modern Screen - June 1964
Actress Mia Farrow was someone who enjoyed hanging out with the Beatles, and her sister was the inspiration for their 1968 song "Dear Prudence." As John Lennon explained it, they were all hanging out with the Maharishi Mahesh Yogi, and "all the people around her were very worried about the girl because she was going insane. So we sang to her."

Module 174: Mia Farrow and Frank Sinatra
Is it significant that Mia Farrow lost her virginity to Frank Sinatra and married him at age 21 (they would marry in 1966)? Or that, as one person who knows her said, "She's too far out"? Considering her very public conflict with Woody Allen, and the fact that she has been famous for over 50 years, do you think that this is the article that Ringo is reading? Why or why not?

The Original Beatles Book - 1964
This fan magazine provides backstories on all of the Beatles as well as a history of Beatlemania in the UK. From the way he's holding the magazine, Paul is probably reading the profile of himself, and so that is the material included in this module.

Module 175: Paul - Handsome and Serious!
What do you think about this "dissection" of the Beatles? Is it just fan hoopla, or does it capture who they are? Why or why not?

Module 176: What They're Saying

Putting the Beatles in context, it's important to know what the music critics of 1964 thought about their music. For example, the *Los Angeles Times* says that "not even their mothers would claim that they sing well." Which source do you feel is the most accurate and/or the most fair?

Superman's Pal Jimmy Olsen

Paul apparently enjoys this series, and who wouldn't?! Superman saves him from a giant octopus!

Module 177: Jimmy Olsen's Pen-Pals

It seems strange today that people would write in questions to a fictional character and have them answered, but 1964 was another time, and people could have a parasocial relationship with a comic book character. Which letter is your favorite? Why? And do you think Twitter serves the same basic purpose in our own time?

16 Scoop! Beatles Complete Story From Birth to Now - 1965

Ringo seems to be enjoying the *16 Scoop!* coverage of the Beatles! While this is from 1965 (luckily, the year can usually be determined by their hairstyles), it provides information not found in other sources of the time.

Module 178: The Beatles Wives and Partners

This is a unique feature in a fan magazine. For this module, research what happened to each of these women, and who ended up married to Eric Clapton.

Module 179: Latest Hot Flashes

This is an update on what the Beatles were up to in 1965, such as John's second collection of nonsensical stories, *A Spaniard in the Works*. How do you believe the tone of Beatles coverage has changed since 1964, or has it changed at all? Regardless, what "hot flash" do you think is the most interesting? Why?

Time Travel Simplified - Conclusions

Module 180: Favorites

Now that you've completed this time travel experience, what were your favorite modules? Which media was your favorite? Why?

Module 181: People

One of the paradoxes of time travel is that while we can return to our own time, the people we read and learn about have to remain in the past. Who made the biggest impression on you in this experience? Who would you like to bring to our time?

Module 182: Change

How has your experience of February 9th 1964 changed you? Has it changed how you see our present time? How has it changed how you see yourself fitting into the greater human experience?

Background Research

In the past decade, the field of psychology has become more interested in time travel. Not like travelling back to December 7th 1972, but something like it. Think about what you did yesterday. Maybe you went out to dinner in a restaurant. Where did you go? What did you have? Who was with you? Or think about your plans for this week. What's on your schedule? Where are you going to be? Who will be with you? Humans have a unique ability to think about the past and plan for the future which sets them apart from the rest of the animal kingdom. This is a process known as *mental time travel* or MTT.

Consider our human ancestors tracking a buffalo on the savannah. They were able to differentiate the hoof of a buffalo from that of an antelope or a zebra. They were also able to tell how "fresh" the print was, whether the buffalo was alone or part of a group, and whether it was healthy or injured. The hunter had to rely on their past experiences to recognize what animal the tracks belonged to and foresee (or as the literature puts it, "pre-live") a future of where the buffalo is going. Even without distance weapons like a bow or a spear, the buffalo could be killed by running it to exhaustion and bludgeoning it to death. Contrast this with the way that lions hunt their prey. A lion will walk right over the tracks of an animal without noticing them. They lack the ability to associate the hoofprint with the prey they are seeking. Instead, lions stalk their prey. They see them, sneak as close as they can, and then charge in order to pounce or knock the animal over. It's the "smash and grab" approach to hunting, and works because most of the prey animals are faster than the lion. This is also why female lions often work together when hunting. But it's very different from the way that humans hunt. Humans are able to hunt the buffalo without ever seeing the buffalo. They know where it has been, and can follow where it is going. Seeing the buffalo after tracking it lets the hunter know that they were correct. This ability to think in terms of the abstraction of "past" and "future" is crucial and determines whether everyone eats or goes hungry. Unlike our animal brethren, we are not trapped in an "eternal present," but can readily recall the past and make plans for the future.

Researchers have conducted studies where they randomly ping people throughout the day to ask about their thoughts and mood. They find that people are three times more likely to be thinking about the future than the past, and when they are thinking about the past, it is as a guide to what they should do in the future. Martin Seligman, one of the founders of the positive psychology movement, goes as far as to say that instead of being called *Homo sapiens* ("wise man"), humans should be referred to as *Homo prospectus*, because plans for the future tend to dominate our thinking.

But let's return to the past for a moment. How stable is it? Let's answer that question with another question: Have you ever been on a hot air balloon ride? This is the paradigm used by researchers Wade, Garry, Read, and Lindsay (2002) to implant false childhood memories in their college student participants. First, they contacted the students' parents in order to obtain family photos from when the student participants were young. They also confirmed with the parents that the student had never been on a hot air balloon ride.

The next step was to use Photoshop to manipulate a photograph to make it look like the student was on a hot air balloon ride with one of their parents when they were a child. The students were then shown this photo, along with three other "true" photos from their childhood. The researchers found that two weeks after looking at the four photos, half of the students were able to remember very specific details about the hot air balloon ride that they had never been on. Many expressed shock when told that the photo was a fake.

Pictures don't lie, except of course when they do.

Other cognitive research has shown that creating a narrative story of an event leads to remembering it better, so Garry and Wade (2005) followed up the original study three years later with a narrative component. In this study, some participants saw the fake picture of themselves on a balloon ride, while others read a detailed narrative story about it. Again, after two weeks, half of the study participants who saw the picture of the balloon ride thought that they had been on a balloon ride as a child; however, 80% of the study participants who read the narrative story believed that they had been on a balloon ride. Why? The researchers believe that in a picture, all of the relevant details can be seen, but in a narrative story, the participants generate their own details about the balloon ride.

So how does all of this relate to creating a time travel experience through the methodology of Time Travel Simplified? First, there is no false implantation of memories - everything that you read about in this book actually happened on or around December 7th 1972. It is mental time travel that allows you to know that 1972 is in the past. Writing out the modules (or even just thinking about them) provides a narrative structure for your critical analysis of the issues of December 7th 1972. Most of the modules ask for your opinion on the material or how it relates to our own time. This act creates a narrative structure for your interaction with the historical past. You don't need to see Photoshopped pictures of yourself at the Paris Peace Talks to understand what happened there! Studies by a number of researchers (Grysman & Hudson, 2010; McLean & Pratt, 2006; Pasupathi, Mansour, & Brubaker, 2007) have shown that "by narrating the personal past and relating it to the present and future self [through mental time travel], people succeed to integrate changes in life and of personality across time" (Köber & Habermas, 2017, p. 608). In other words, what the Time Travel Simplified methodology does is create an understanding of a specific moment in the historical past, and relates it to the present (and future) self, allowing us to integrate that information into our life and our personality. As I wrote in the introduction, the real paradox of time travel is not that it changes the past - it's that it changes you in the present (and the future). After completing all of the modules, not only do you understand the past, you understand how we got to this particular present, and most importantly, you understand yourself - your hopes, fears, biases, influences, and ways of seeing the world - in an entirely new way. Time travel, at its core, is about human potential and personal growth.

I believe that the best analogy for the changes created by Time Travel Simplified is a "study abroad" experience. In both experiences you are taken out of your usual time and place and put in a foreign country where you have to understand how "they do things differently there" (to paraphrase the L.P. Hartley quote which begins this book). And the benefits of both experiences are very much the same. They both let us "see the world," whether it is a different culture in our own time or our own culture in an earlier time. They both provide an education in a new culture, allowing us to understand what is acceptable and what issues are important. They both allow us to discover new interests that can be pursued after returning from the experience. They both provide a shared experience with people who have gone through the same thing - we're now all a part of a Society of Time Travelers! Both experiences provide the opportunity for personal growth, allowing us to examine our beliefs in a new light through a different context. Finally, both provide a life experience like none other.

This book, and the series that it is a part of, are the culmination of research which I've been conducting over the past few years. What I have attempted to accomplish is the creation of a time travel experience that anyone can be a part of, no matter their age or knowledge of history.

That's why I'm willing to guarantee that "It's time travel, or it's free." Why would you know SO MUCH about one particular day from the past if you hadn't been there before? And you HAVE! Six months from now the memories you've formed from this experience will integrate with the knowledge you already have and become a memory from your personal past, like a study abroad experience.

So about that guarantee. If you have purchased the book, completed all of the modules, waited six months, and don't feel that you have experienced what it would be like to time travel, then I am happy to reimburse you. The details for reimbursement are available on timetravelsimplified.com.

I stand by the methodology I've developed with Time Travel Simplified because I know that it works and has changed me for the better. I sincerely hope that you have enjoyed the experience too. Thank you for joining me on this journey!

Research References

Bluck, S., Alea, N., & Ali, S. (2014). Remembering the historical roots of remembering the personal past. *Applied Cognitive Psychology, 28*, 290-300. http://doi.org/fpjk

Brewin, C. R., & Andrews, B. (2017). Creating memories for false autobiographical events in childhood: A systematic review. *Applied Cognitive Psychology, 31*, 2-23. http://doi.org/dtb5

Corballis, M. C. (2013). Wandering tales: Evolutionary origins of mental time travel and language. *Frontiers in Psychology, 4*, 1-8.

Garry, M., & Gerrie, M. P. (2005). When photographs create false memories. *Current Directions in Psychological Science, 14*(6), 321-325.

Garry, M., & Wade, K. A. (2005). Actually, a picture is worth less than 45 words: Narratives produce more false memories than photographs do. *Psychonomic Bulletin and Review, 12*(2), 359-366.

Grysman, A., & Hudson, J. A. (2010). Abstracting and extracting: Causal coherence and the development of the life story. *Memory, 18*(6), 565-580.

Hardt, R. (2018). Storytelling agents: Why narrative rather than mental time travel is fundamental. *Phenomenology and the Cognitive Sciences, 17*, 535-554. http://doi.org/dtb3

Hessen-Kayfitz, J., Scoboria, A., & Nespoli, K. (2017). The labeling of photos when suggesting false childhood events can enhance or suppress false memory formation. *Psychology of Consciousness: Theory, Research, and Practice, 4*(3), 288-297.

Köber, C., & Habermas, T. (2017). How stable is the personal past? Stability of most important autobiographical memories and life narratives across eight years in a life span sample. *Journal of Personality and Social Psychology, 113*(4), 608-626.

Liester, M. B., & Sullivan, E. E. (2019). A review of epigenetics in human consciousness. *Cogent Psychology, 6*, 1-29.

McAdams, D. P. (2001). The psychology of life stories. *Review of General Psychology, 5*(2), 100-122.

McLean, K. C., & Pratt, M. W. (2006). Life's little (and big) lessons: Identity statuses and meaning-making in the turning point narratives of emerging adults. *Developmental Psychology, 42*(4), 714-722.

Otgaar, H., Scororia, A., & Smeets, T. (2013). Experimentally evoking nonbelieved memories for childhood events. *Journal of Experimental Psychology: Learning, Memory, and Cognition, 39*(3), 717-730.

Pasupathi, M., Mansour, E., & Brubaker, J. (2007). Developing a life story: Constructing relations between self and experience in autobiographical narratives. *Human Development, 50*(2-3) 85-110. http://doi.org/dxc2dr

Pezdek, K. & Blandon-Gitlin, I. (2017). It is just harder to construct memories for false autobiographical events. *Applied Cognitive Psychology, 31*, 42-44.

Rasmussen, K. W., & Berntsen, D. (2014). "I can see clearly now": The effect of cue imageability on mental time travel. *Memory & Cognition, 42*(7), 1063-1075.

Sanson, M., Newman, E. J., & Garry, M. (2018). The characteristics of directive future experiences and directive memories. *Psychology of Consciousness: Theory, Research, and Practice, 5*(3), 278-294.

Scoboria, A., Wysman, L., & Otgaar, H. (2012). Credible suggestions affect false autobiographical beliefs. *Memory, 20*(3), 429-442.

Seligman, M. E., & Roepke, A. M. (2016). Prospection gone awry: Depression. In M. E. Seligman, P. Railton, R. F. Butler, & C. Sripada (Eds.), *Homo prospectus* (pp. 281-304). Oxford University Press.

Seligman, M. E., & Tierney, J. (2017, May 19). We aren't built to live in the moment. *The New York Times*, https://www.nytimes.com/2017/05/19/opinion/sunday/why-the-future-is-always-on-your-mind.html

Storm, B. C., & Jobe, T. A. (2012). Remembering the past and imagining the future: Examining the consequences of mental time travel on memory. *Memory, 20*(3), 224-235.

Wade, K. A., Garry, M., Read, J. D., & Lindsay, D. S. (2002). A picture is worth a thousand lies: Using false photographs to create false childhood memories. *Psychonomic Bulletin & Review, 9*, 597-603.

One Last Thing . . .

I want to thank you for buying this book and participating in this time travel experience. If you enjoyed it, I would appreciate you leaving positive feedback in whatever venue that you choose. Your experience will help others make a decision on whether to choose this book, so feedback is important.

If you would like to support my research on time travel, there are at least two ways that you can help. First, I have a Patreon account for Time Travel Simplified which allows you to financially support my work and in turn receive additional print and video media with their corresponding modules. It's also an easy way to interact with me on what you'd like to see and to find out what I'm working on. Second, if you are interested in participating in psychological research about time travel, then contact me at my Truman State University email. I'm easy to find online - I'm the Mark Hatala who is a college professor, and NOT the one who is the dentist or the golf pro.

I will close by saying that if you are able to physically travel back through time to February 9th 1964, please visit my family at my childhood home at 6297 Denison Blvd., Parma Heights, Ohio. My parents are Paul and Dorothy. They are good people and will welcome you. Their phone number is 216-885-0165, but you don't need to call before you stop by. I won't be born for another two years, but you can visit with my sister and brother. See you then!

Sunday February 9, 1964

Morning

6:00 ⑤ **ARTHRITIS TELETHON**
[SPECIAL] The ninth annual telethon for the benefit of the Southern California Chapter, Arthritis and Rheumatism Foundation is presented live until 6 P.M. Among those expected to appear: Jack Benny, Bob Hope, Lawrence Welk, and Andy Williams. Johnny Grant is host.

6:45 ② **GIVE US THIS DAY**—Religion

6:50 ② **NEWS**

7:00 ② **LAMP UNTO MY FEET**
"Race, the Church and Higher Education," a panel discussion on church efforts to improve minority group opportunities.
　④ **MR. WIZARD**—Science
　⑪ **WHITE HUNTER**—Adventure
"The Valley of the Dead."

7:15 ⑧ **LIGHT TIME**—Religion

7:30 ② **LOOK UP AND LIVE**-Religion
Is our present concept of religion out of date? Dietrich Bonhoeffer, a Lutheran pastor, threw this stiff query at Protestant theologians before his execution by the Nazis. Portions of his letters and diaries, written while in prison, are read by David Hooks.
　④ [COLOR] **DAVEY AND GOLIATH**—Religion
　⑧ **CHRISTOPHER PROGRAM**
　⑩ **HOUSE OF HAPPINESS**
　⑪ **HIGHWAY PATROL**—Police
Chief Mathews attempts to capture a husband and wife. Broderick Crawford.

7:45 ④ [COLOR] **LET'S TALK ABOUT**
　⑧ **ADVENTURES IN FARMING**
　⑩ **DAVEY AND GOLIATH**
　⑬ **CHRISTOPHER PROGRAM**
"Reassess Your Values."

8:00 ② **CAMERA THREE**
"Colette by Others," first of two shows, features novelists Katherine Anne Porter and Glenway Wescott in a discussion of the 20th-century French author's life and work. James Macandrew is host.
　④ **MOVIE**—Drama
"Flaxy Martin." (1949) A young lawyer becomes involved with an unscrupulous show girl and a mobster. Virginia Mayo, Dorothy Malone. (90 min.)

⑤ **TELETHON**—Continued
[SPECIAL] See 6 A.M., Ch. 5. (Live)
⑧ **LAMP UNTO MY FEET**
See 7 A.M., Ch. 2, for details.
⑨ **BABYSITTER**—Children
⑩ **HERALD OF TRUTH**—Relig
⑪ **GREAT CHURCHES**—Relig
The Rev. William H. Ilten presides services at St. John's Lutheran Church Montebello.
⑬ **GOSPEL HOUR**—Music

8:30 ② **LIGHT OF FAITH**—Religio
Father Michael Dunne guests.
　⑥ **MOVIE**—Double Feature
1. "The Fighting Gringo." (1939) Geo O'Brien. 2. "Desert Passage." Tim H Joan Dixon. (Three hours, 30 min.)
　⑦ **SUNDAY MORNING CHAP**
　⑧ **LOOK UP AND LIVE**-Relig
See 7:30 A.M., Ch. 2, for details.
　⑩ **HOUR OF ST. FRANCIS**

9:00 ② **LEARNING '64**—Education
Phil Essman talks about blind teach
　⑦ **MOVIE**—Western
"Angel and the Badman." (1947) J Wayne, Gail Russell. (Two hours)
　⑧ **CAMERA THREE**
See 8 A.M., Ch. 2 for details.
　⑨ **MOVIE**—Western
"Comanche." (1956) An Indian scout t to negotiate a peace treaty. Dana drews, Kent Smith. (90 min.)
　⑩ **PRODUCT PREVIEW**—Lon
　⑪ **MOVIE**—Musical Comedy
"Rise and Shine." (1941) Musical com on a college campus. Jack Oakie, Li Darnell, George Murphy. (Two hours)
　⑬ **VARIEDADES**-Roberto Igle

9:30 ② **DISCOVERING ART**—Mans
"What Gustave Eiffel Did for Paris."
　④ **CHRISTOPHER PROGRAM**
"Emphasize Sound Values." The neces of implanting a sense of values.
　⑧ **FACE THE NATION**-Interv
　⑩ **PROFILE**—San Diego State
See Sat. 2:30 P.M., Ch. 4, for deta

10:00 ② **MOVIE**—Comedy
"Cafe Metropole." (1937) A play poses as a Russian prince in order win an American heiress. Loretta Yo Tyrone Power, Adolphe Menjou. (90 m

(3) MOVIE—Comedy
"Father Was a Fullback." (1949) A football team has a habit of losing. Fred MacMurray. (Two hours)

(4) THIS IS THE LIFE—Religion
"Beautiful Morning."

(5) TELETHON—Continued
SPECIAL See 6 A.M., Ch. 5. (Live)

(8) LET THERE BE LIGHT

(10) IT IS WRITTEN—Religion
COLOR "Touch and Live."

(13) PANORAMA LATINO

10:30 (4) (10) FRONTIERS OF FAITH
In "Moses: The Law-Giver," Dr. Hagen Staack describes Moses' relationship to God, and how it enabled the prophet to lead his people.

(8) MOVIE—Western
"Hangman's Knot." (1952) After capturing a shipment of gold bullion from Union soldiers, a band of Confederates learn the war is over. Randolph Scott. (90 min.)

(9) LADIES OF THE PRESS
Franklin D. Roosevelt Jr. guests.

(13) FAITH FOR TODAY—Religion
COLOR "Silent Is the Moon."

11:00 (4) MOVIE—Western
"Colorado Territory." (1949) A notorious bandit decides to quit his gang after one more hold-up. Joel McCrea, Virginia Mayo, Dorothy Malone. (90 min.)

(7) DISCOVERY '64—Children
How does man deal with "The Forces of Nature?" Using three examples, the volcano, the hurricane and water power, host Frank Buxton and science teacher Steve Fischer show how science warns us of the first two—and harnesses the third.

(9) MOVIE—Musical
"Let's Be Happy." See Saturday 12 Noon, Ch. 9, for details. (One hour, 55 min.)

(10) TEACHER '64—Education
Teacher Lloyd Otterman and his students demonstrate physical fitness.

(11) WONDERAMA—Children

(13) CHURCH IN THE HOME

11:30 (2) SUM AND SUBSTANCE
Theologian Paul Tillich guests today.

(7) PRESS CONFERENCE
Rose Blyth of the newly authorized educational station KCET-TV guests.

(10) KOGO'S CORNER—Clark

February 9, 1964 **Sunday**

Afternoon-Evening

⑬ ROBIN HOOD—Adventure
"The Secret Pool." Sir Cedric Hayworth can't smell a fishy deal when Robin Hood bargains with him. Richard Greene.

4:30 ⑧ EXHIBITION TENNIS
[SPECIAL] From the Kona Kai Club on Shelter Island comes a live tennis exhibition featuring top pro stars including Jack Kramer, Pancho Gonzales, Tony Trabert and Ted Schroeder. Lyle Bond hosts.

⑬ MOVIE—Comedy
"The Boogie Men Will Get You." (1942) A string of corpses are kept in a wine cellar. Boris Karloff. (90 min.)

5:00 ② ⑧ ALUMNI FUN
For the University of Minnesota: Sen. Hubert H. Humphrey (D., Minn.); actress Arlene Dahl; and Dr. Charles W. Mayo, director of the Mayo Clinic. For the University of Cincinnati: Dodgers pitcher Sandy Koufax; actor Lee Bowman; and Rear Adm. Edward C. Kenney, surgeon geenral of the U.S. Navy. Clifton Fadiman.

③ ⑦ TRAILMASTER—Western
Flint, mixed up in a horse theft, is tried and found guilty by Hale. Sam Upton: Nick Adams. Flint: Robert Horton. Hale: John McIntire. (60 min.)

④ ⑩ RETURN TO OZ
[SPECIAL] [COLOR] In this new musical-cartoon version of L. Frank Baum's classic fantasy "The Wizard of Oz," Dorothy returns to the strange land, her friends — and the Wicked Witch. (60 min.)

Voices

Dorothy...............Susan Conway
Dandy Lion, Wizard.......Carl Bannis
Socrates.................Alfie Scopp
Rusty...................Larry Mann
Munchkins..............Susan Morse
Glinda ....Pegi Loder

⑨ MOVIE—Western
"Dodge City." (1939) A two-fisted marshal sets out to clean up Dodge City. Errol Flynn, Ann Sheridan. (90 min.)

⑪ MOVIE—Science Fiction
"The Lost Missile." (1958) New Yorkers have little more than an hour left to live as a radioactive missile circles the earth. Robert Loggia, Larry Kerr. (90 min.)

5:30 ② AMATEUR HOUR—Ted Mack
Ted Mack's guests include accordionist James McCauley, baton twirler Susan Janick, soprano Bonnie Fugarino, and songstress Cheri Lee.

⑧ NEWS, WEATHER, SPORTS

Evening

6:00 ② ③ ⑧ TWENTIETH CENTURY—Documentary
"The Songs of Harold Arlen." Tony Bennett — recording Arlen's latest song—

5 POLKA PARADE—Sinclair

6 SAM BENEDICT—Drama

7 MOVIE—Melodrama

"Cat Girl." (1957) L.A. TV Debut. A woman who believes she's under the curse of the leopard suspects her husband of infidelity. Barbara Shelley, Robert Ayres, Kay Callard, Paddy Webster. (90 min.)

10 NEWS

13 [COLOR] ROCKY AND HIS FRIENDS—Cartoons

6:30 **4** BIOGRAPHY—Documentary

Plunged into darkness before she was two by an illness which left her deaf and blind, Helen Keller has lived in a world of light created by her enthusiasm for everything around her. Mike Wallace.

9 MAVERICK—Western

"Ghost Rider." Bret befriends a young widow. Bret: James Garner. Mary Shane: Joanna Barnes. (60 min.)

10 [COLOR] OUTDOOR SPORTSMAN—Al Couppee

11 MOVIE—Drama

"Border Incident." (1949) The U.S. and Mexican immigration authorities combine forces to fight smugglers. Ricardo Montalban, George Murphy. (90 min.)

13 [COLOR] ROD ROCKET

7:00 **2** **8** LASSIE—Drama

In this second of five episodes, Lassie is rescued and cared for by a forest ranger. Timmy: Jon Provost. Ruth: June Lockhart. Paul: Hugh Reilly. Corey: Robert Bray.

3 OZZIE AND HARRIET—Comedy

June offers to substitute for Dave's vacationing secretary, and Dave can't think of a way to turn her down. The Nelsons portray themselves. June: June Blair.

4 BILL DANA—Comedy

"Eddie Gets Fired" when he gallantly takes the blame for one of José's blunders. José: Bill Dana. Eddie: Gary Crosby. Phillips: Jonathan Harris.

5 MOVIE—Drama

[COLOR] "Desiree." (1954) The daughter of a Marseilles silk merchant meets an impoverished general named Napoleon Bonaparte. Marlon Brando, Jean Simmons, Merle Oberon. (Two hours)

6 PROBE—Dr. Albert E. Burke

Natalie Wood; Skip Homeier. (Two hours)

8:00 **2** **8** **ED SULLIVAN—Variety**
England's rock 'n' rolling Beatles make
their American television debut, and 30
policeman will be on hand in case a
"Beatle-mania" reaches the riot pitch —
as it has in England. Other scheduled
guests include "Oliver!" star Georgia
Brown and the show's youngsters singing
"Consider Yourself" and other "Oliver!"
tunes; Tessie O'Shea of Broadway's "Girl
Who Came to Supper"; and actor-impres-
sionist Frank Gorshin, postponed from last
week. Ray Bloch orchestra. (60 min.)

www.ingramcontent.com/pod-product-compliance
Lightning Source LLC
Chambersburg PA
CBHW051345020726
47501CB00007B/2273